D1040161

Crushing It

Crushing It

JOANNE LEVY

ALADDIN MIX

New York London Toronto Sydney New Delhi

ALADDIN M!X

Simon & Schuster Children's Publishing Division

1230 Avenue of the Americas, New York, New York 10020

First Aladdin M!X edition January 2017

Text copyright © 2017 by Simon & Schuster, Inc.

Cover illustration copyright © 2017 by Angela Li

Also available in an Aladdin hardcover edition.

All rights reserved, including the right of reproduction in whole or in part in any form.

ALADDIN and related logo are registered trademarks of Simon & Schuster, Inc.

ALADDIN M!X and related logo are registered trademarks of Simon & Schuster, Inc.

For information about special discounts for bulk purchases, please contact

Simon & Schuster Special Sales at 1-866-506-1949 or business@simonandschuster.com.

The Simon & Schuster Speakers Bureau can bring authors to your live event. For more information or to book an event contact the Simon & Schuster Speakers Bureau at 1-866-248-3049 or visit our website at www.simonspeakers.com.

Book designed by Laura Lyn DiSiena

The text of this book was set in Palatino.

Manufactured in the United States of America 1216 OFF

10 9 8 7 6 5 4 3 2 1

Library of Congress Cataloging-in-Publication Data

Names: Levy, Joanne, author.

Title: Crushing it / by Joanne Levy.

Description: Aladdin M!X edition. | New York : Aladdin M!X, 2016. | Summary: Middle school is bad enough for braces-wearing, manga-loving, uncoordinated Kat, but helping her two best friends get together will mean that Kat has no chance of winning Tyler's affection for herself.

Identifiers: LCCN 2015042245 | ISBN 9781481464734 (pbk) | ISBN 9781481464741 (hc) | ISBN 9781481464758 (eBook)

Subjects: | CYAC: Middle schools—Fiction. | Schools—Fiction. | Best friends—Fiction. | Friendship—Fiction. | Cousins—Fiction. | Self-esteem—Fiction.

Classification: LCC PZ7.L58323 Cru 2016 | DDC [Fic]—dc23

LC record available at https://lccn.loc.gov/2015042245

For my dad, Dan Levy, and in loving memory of my mom, Marcia Levy, two people who really crushed it at that parenting thing

Chapter 1

MY STOMACH GROWLED SO LOUDLY, I WAS SURE other kids could hear it in the school hallway. It was lunchtime, and obviously I was starving, but as Olivia and I walked toward the caf, we got stopped. Again. This time it was by one of Olivia's eighth-grade dance-team friends to talk about their last rehearsal.

"You were so awesome," the girl said, looking at Olivia with wide, awestruck eyes. "You were like a *gazelle* out there."

My cousin and best friend—or "best cousin," a term we thought up when we were seven—was a *gazelle*. And apparently, everyone *loved* gazelles around this place.

In the two weeks since we'd started seventh grade, Olivia had been propelled into middle-school superstardom. She'd grown like a foot over the summer; she had long, flowing blond hair, and her beautiful clothes always seemed to check off the "cool" boxes with zero effort.

I guess I shouldn't have been too surprised about the superstardom thing. I mean, she'd always been the graceful one, the pretty and popular one, with her shiny smile and outgoing personality. Her bubbly nature and the way she got so excited about things were what everyone—including me—loved about her. So it was just a matter of time before she became seventh grade's official *it* girl.

Oh, and did I mention she'd made it onto the dance team, which seventh graders almost never get on? Because she's *a gazelle*. I hadn't even bothered trying out, because with my glasses, braces, and two left feet, I am about as graceful as a warthog. *No one* wants to see that.

I know it probably sounds like I'm all snark talking about Olivia, but it's not that way at all. She is kind and funny, and I do love her, not just because we're family, although that's how we became friends in the first place. Our dads are brothers, and with us being almost the same age, it was like we were born to be friends. So of course we love each other, even if we haven't always had a ton of stuff in common.

It wasn't her fault she's beautiful and graceful and everything I'm not. And anyway, being her friend was sort of like being superstar-adjacent.

The eighth grader went on. "I swear, I have *never* seen anyone pick up routines so quickly! You are *so* talented, Olivia. There has probably *never* been anyone as good as you. Ever!"

I fought the urge to roll my eyes. Because while I knew Olivia was good, she wasn't like *Dancing with the Stars* good. This fangirl was being over the top, and I was beginning to get crabby.

My stomach let out another monstrous gurgle. I needed food soon, but if Olivia didn't hurry up, we'd never get to eat before lunch period was over.

"Livvy," I said, trying to drag her away from the other girl, who was going on *and on* about dancing and was using a bunch of French-sounding words that I didn't understand. "Can we go, please?"

Olivia smiled down at me and said, "Yeah, just a sec."

But I couldn't wait any longer. I reached into my lunch bag and pulled out the first thing I touched, which was a hard-boiled egg. An *egg*. Not even peeled.

Sigh.

When Dad had handed me my bag as I was leaving the house, I should have realized it was going to be bad. Since he'd started his new vet practice a few months before, we almost never saw him. When we did, he was either an exhausted zombie or scatter-brained and in a rush.

My older sister, Laura, was supposed to make lunches. But that morning, after Mom had left for work, Laura and Dad had gotten in a huge fight, and before making mine, she'd stormed off—which was getting to be standard behavior these days. So while I was in the shower, Dad had apparently grabbed some random stuff and thrown it in my bag.

I couldn't exactly peel an egg in the hallway, so I dropped it back in the bag, scared to look at what else was in there. Olivia was going to get one more minute before I'd leave her in the hallway.

As I looked up at the clock so I could time her, I noticed a sign for our upcoming dance: the Fall Ball.

I snorted at the thought. Right. Like I'd be going to *that*. Not only did I not have a clue *how* to dance, but no one would ever ask me *to* dance, so why sign up for that kind of humiliation?

"What's so funny?" Olivia asked, coming up beside me. I guess she was done with her dance-team groupie.

I nodded toward the sign.

Olivia squealed and clapped her hands. "Oh! I was wondering when our first dance would be. Doesn't the 'Fall Ball' sound so *elegant*? I can't wait."

Elegant? "You're not planning on going, are you?" I asked, which was stupid, because obviously she was.

She looked at me like I had asked her the answer to a particularly difficult math problem. "What do you mean? *Of course* I'm going. Mom promised me she'd take me shopping for the perfect dress for our first dance. And I'm going to get my hair and nails done too. Aren't *you* going?"

I started walking toward the caf. "Nah, I don't think so. But you have a good time."

"Wait," she said, stopping in the hallway. "You're not coming?"

"To the Fall Ball? Not a chance," I said with another snort.

"Why not?" Olivia asked like it was a huge shock to her that I might not want to go. Like she couldn't possibly understand why *anyone* wouldn't want to go.

"Can we please discuss this while we're eating?" I asked, sure that my stomach was starting to eat some of my other organs and worried I might lose something I needed.

Olivia started walking again. "Fine. But first I need your opinion on something."

"If it's what to wear to the dance, I'm obviously the wrong person to ask," I said, pointing down at my hoodie and jeans.

"It's not that," Olivia said as we got to the cafeteria. "Hold on. It's too noisy to talk. Over here," she said, pointing to a rectangular table with a few empty seats at the end. I dropped my bag on the table and sat down across from her. She dug into her backpack for her lunch and set it on the table. Then she looked at me very intently.

"Okay, so . . . ," I said, fidgeting because she was staring at me but not saying anything.

"Yeah," she finally said, pulling her sandwich out of her bag and taking a bite. "I was hoping you could help me . . ."

Before she got any further, a body landed heavily in the chair next to me, scaring me half to death. No, maybe three-quarters to death. As I gasped, I turned my head to see who it was, but I shouldn't have been surprised.

"Tyler!" I scolded, although I was only sort of mad. He was my other best friend, after all.

I mean, he was *kind of* my other best friend. More like my next-door neighbor who I'd known my entire life. The person I'd always climbed trees and talked books with; my partner in annihilating zombies on Xbox.

Except we hadn't played in a while, since he'd been away for the summer at wilderness camp. I was eager to show him the new moves that were going to let me totally kick his butt in the game. Although the couple of times he'd invited me over, I'd been busy.

Sort of. At least, that's what I'd told him.

"Hey, Kat," he said with a smile, then looked across the table at Olivia.

"Hi, Tyler," she said in a very odd voice. I glanced over at her, and she was smiling really wide at him. Maybe she'd noticed he was different this year too. Of course she had; how could she not? He had changed so much.

They didn't know each other that well, because while Olivia and I had always gone to school together, Tyler had gone to a private academy since kindergarten. He and I played together on weekends or after school. This year was going to be totally different, though; his parents had decided to put him in public school with us, which I'd been excited about.

At first. Until he returned home from camp and I saw him for the first time and almost didn't recognize him. My stomach had started doing flip-flops because he was . . . different. I couldn't figure out exactly what it was, but something inside me told me things were weird. Not that he was *acting* differently; just, he made me nervous. Like I wanted to be around him and *not* be around him at the same time.

"Hi, Olivia," Tyler said politely. Then he turned to me. "So, Zombie Slashers tonight?"

"I . . ."

I wanted to, I really did, but something in me was scared to sit next to him on a couch. It mostly had to do with the fact that he'd gotten taller and tanned and his hair had grown longer and fell into his eyes, making him look a little . . . I guess "mysterious" is the right word. I'd never worried before about how I acted around him, but suddenly I couldn't think of what I should say. I was sure I'd blurt out stupid things. Things like how his hair was mysterious.

"I can't. I have too much homework, and if we're starting at the shelter this weekend, I can't fall behind this week."

He nodded. "Good call."

"Starting at the shelter?" Olivia asked, her eyes on Tyler.

"We're volunteering at the animal shelter," I said. "The one where my dad is their volunteer vet a couple of Sundays a month. We'll be walking dogs and that kind of thing. We start this weekend."

"Oh, that sounds amazing," she said, and then tossed her long hair over her shoulder.

Tyler looked at her funny, but she kept smiling at him, her non-braces-covered teeth practically beaming at him. I pressed my lips together and looked down at my lunch bag, suddenly not as hungry as I had been. I pushed the bag away, not even bothering to find out what was in there.

Tyler grabbed it, opened it up, and looked inside. "What *is* this?"

I glanced over at him. He was smirking at me, his hair falling over his forehead until he pushed it back with his hand. The move made my stomach roll over. Seriously, I had to look away. What was *happening* to me?

I cleared my throat. "My dad's culinary disaster," I said.

"Aren't you going to eat any of it?"

I shrugged. "I don't even know what's in there."

He frowned. "Why are you talking funny?"

"I'm not," I said.

"You're not moving your lips," Olivia said helpfully. "Is there something wrong with your braces?"

So much for *not* drawing attention to my braces. To distract from my suddenly hot face, I grabbed my lunch bag and dumped the contents onto the table. "I'm fine," I said.

Tyler reached for the oatmeal-raisin cookies and took them. He didn't even have to ask, because, unlike my father, *he* knows I hate oatmeal-raisin. And unlike me, he *loves* oatmeal-raisin. It's actually his favorite.

I took stock of the rest of my lunch and sighed, grabbing the apple and ignoring the rest. At least Dad had remembered to cut it up so I could eat it with my braces.

"Sardines?" Tyler said, grinning as he held up the square can.

I rolled my eyes. "Like I said: Dad. Help yourself to whatever else."

Tyler grabbed the egg and looked into the empty bag. "No salt?"

I shook my head.

He got up from his chair. "Right back."

He was barely away from the table when Olivia leaned toward me. *"That's* what I need your opinion on," she whispered.

"If eggs need salt?"

She gave me a *Really?* look. "No, duh. *Tyler.* You know him really well. What's the best way to ask him to the dance?"

I understood every word she was saying, but when she put them all together like that, they seemed to stall out my brain. "Huh?"

"I want to go to the dance with him."

"Tyler," I said, just to be sure. *"Tyler Lot?* The guy who was just sitting here."

"Yeah," she said, nodding and looking out over my shoulder. "He'll be back in a second, but . . . he got *seriously cute* over the summer. Don't you think?"

I shrugged and put a slice of apple in my mouth so I wouldn't blurt out anything about mysterious hair. "I dthon't know," I mumbled through apple chunks.

"He did," she said. "Trust me. He's now the most adorable guy in our grade, and with him being new here . . . well, I'm sure you've heard all the girls talking about *the cute new guy.*"

I *had* heard the other girls talking about Tyler like that. And at first I'd thought it was funny that they were all giggling and whispering about him—my next-door best friend since forever. But then I kind of hated all the attention he was getting. And now Olivia?

I chewed the apple and looked at her. She was so beautiful, with her long shiny hair and white teeth. Not to mention her pretty blue eyes and gazellelike dancing abilities. She was the whole package. Except . . .

"I'm not really sure he's your type," I said, trying to be nice about it.

She pouted. "What do you mean? You don't think he'd like me?"

"No, not that at all!" I said quickly, hating that I'd hurt her feelings. "He's just really into gaming and comics and stuff. You know that."

They didn't know each other that well, since she was more my at-school and family-event friend and he was more my weekend and *after*-school friend (until this year). But many times in the past, she'd rolled her eyes when I'd told her I was going to play Xbox with him or we were going to a superhero movie. She'd never been interested in that stuff or asked to play with us.

She shrugged. "So? Haven't you ever heard that opposites attract?"

I sighed, having a feeling where this was going. "Yeah."

"Well," she said with wide eyes, like that was explanation enough. "How should I ask him?"

Something inside me wanted to tell her she *shouldn't* ask him. Because, honestly, I couldn't see them going to the dance together.

Or maybe secretly I didn't want him to go to the dance with *anyone* because I wouldn't be going. But she was my best cousin, and she was looking at me very seriously, and I could tell this was really important to her.

"Kat? What do you think? How should I ask him?"

I answered her truthfully. "I have no idea."

She pursed her lips and glanced behind me again. "Oh. He's coming back. Maybe you can talk to him for me. Go play Zombie Killers with him tonight and get some intel."

"Zombie Slashers," I corrected.

She rolled her eyes. "Whatever. Just do it for me? Please? *Pretty* please? I'll owe you huge."

Looking at her, I knew any guy would be crazy to not want to go to the dance with her. No guy, not even my best guy friend, would ever want to go to the dance with *me*. Because guys like gazelles, not warthogs. I'd never be graceful or tall, and I still had glasses and braces and was into gaming and graphic novels. I might not have had much dating experience, but I was no dummy: Boys like girls like Olivia—girly girls who know how to dress and dance and put on makeup.

I felt my throat get dry and tight, and I looked down at the can of sardines, reading the ingredients (sardines and oil) so I wouldn't have to look at her.

Finally, when I'd learned that there were nineteen grams of protein per can of sardines (still not reason enough to eat them), I figured at least one of us should get what she wanted. And maybe if she went to the dance with him, things could go back to normal for Tyler and me.

"Okay. Fine," I said. "I'll talk to him."

She did a tiny clap in her seat and then schooled her face. "Okay, shhhh, he's coming back," she said, even though I wasn't even talking.

Tyler sat down again, dropping two salt packets on the table before grabbing the egg and starting to peel. "Geez. What kind of school is this? I had to ask, like, three lunch ladies where the salt was."

". . . as I was saying, your dance squad. So when's your next practice?" I said, so Tyler wouldn't know we'd been talking about him.

Olivia glanced over at Tyler and then back at me, obviously confused. "What?"

Tyler looked up. Now *he* was confused. "Huh?"

Oh, jeez. I turned to Tyler, realizing I needed to change the subject. Fast. "It turns out I don't have that much homework after all. See you after dinner?"

"Yeah, cool," he said. "That'll be great."

"Can't wait," I lied.

Chapter 2

I'D GRABBED A SNACK WHEN I'D GOTTEN HOME from school, but if I'd known dinner was going to be so late, I would have eaten more. Like a whole pot roast or something.

"Can't we just eat?" Laura whined as she came into the kitchen.

I was sitting at the little desk working on my manga, *Hector: Ninja Cat*, based on my own cat (Hector, obviously). It had started out as an art project last year, but when I'd gotten an A on it and had shown part of it to Tyler, he'd said I should make it into a whole novel. The cat in my book did a lot more ninja-ing and a lot less sleeping than the real one. Still, making a graphic novel about a cat with crazy ninja skills combined two of my favorite things: drawing and animals. Oh, and ninja stuff, so I guess that made it three of my favorite things.

I glanced up at my sister. As annoying as she was, I was very interested in Mom's answer, so I turned and looked over to where she was standing near the stove with her cell phone in her hand.

She let out a long breath, something she did a lot when talking to Laura these days. "Your father just texted that he is on his way. We eat dinner as a family, Laura."

"It's almost seven o'clock," Laura pointed out. I looked at the microwave clock; she was right. Whoa, later than I'd realized.

"Look," Mom said, putting her phone down, crossing her arms, and leaning back against the counter. "You both know Dad's working very hard. His practice is brand-new, and he *told* us he was going to have to work a lot to get it off the ground. He's under a lot of pressure to make that happen, so we need to be supportive."

"I would be more supportive on a full stomach," Laura muttered.

"What's that?" Mom said in *that* tone, which meant she'd heard every word.

"Ugh! Nothing!" Laura said, and stormed out of the room.

Mom just stared after her.

"Teenagers, huh?" I said.

Mom looked at me and gave me a little smile. "I am sorry, but . . ." She sighed again. "He should be home any minute."

I nodded, although I wasn't sure even *she* believed it. Because he was late *every* night. I understood he was busy and worked hard, but I also saw where Laura was coming from, because we were hungry. And sometimes it felt like when Dad *did* come home, he just complained about the vet office. The food reps this; the surgical supplier that; the vet tech called in sick; the photocopier broke. Blah. Blah. Blah.

I was about to turn back to my drawing when my cell phone buzzed in my pocket. I pulled it out.

Tyler: *You coming over?*

Shoot. At this rate it would be bedtime before we ate, which meant I wasn't going to be able to hang out with him. Although I was kind of relieved about that, I *had* promised Olivia I would feel him out about the dance.

I turned to Mom. "How long, do you think?"

She shrugged. "Ten minutes, maybe?"

I got up out of the chair. "I promised Tyler I'd come over tonight to play Zombie Slashers, but I guess that's not going to happen. I'll just run over and tell him. I'll be right back."

She looked at me sideways. "You're not going to start the game and disappear are you? I want you here when we're ready to eat."

My stomach growled like *it* wanted to answer her. "Don't worry, Mom. I'll be right back."

"Okay. If Dad happens to pull up before you're back, I'll text you."

I nodded as I patted the pocket that held my phone and jogged toward the door.

Chapter 3

MRS. LOT OPENED THE DOOR AND SMILED AT ME. "Hi, Kat," she said. "He's down in the basement."

"Thanks," I said, returning her smile. I went down the hallway and made the three turns that took me to the stairs to the basement. I could hear he was playing already, but I needed a second to prepare myself. Why was my gastrointestinal system having so much trouble with the idea of being around Tyler? Is it possible to have a stomach flu just from being around one particular person?

Stop being ridiculous, Kat, I told myself. I took a few deep breaths and started down the stairs.

Halfway down, I was able to see him sitting there on the sofa, leaning forward with his elbows on his knees. He was so focused on the screen that he didn't notice me. It gave me a second to look him over, which confirmed what my internal plumbing had already figured out: I had it for this guy. My best guy friend who I'd known forever. The guy who had gone away for the summer and had come back so cute that it almost hurt to look at him.

The guy who was currently beheading a zombie.

Yeah, I had it for him *bad*.

But as I looked at him, I thought about Olivia and how she had it for him too. Olivia the gazelle. Kat the warthog.

He would never go for me in a million years. Sure, I was his friend, and obviously that hadn't changed over the summer, but he would never look at me *that way*. No one wants to date the warthog. Better to just get him and Olivia together, and I'd lose this stupid crush on him, which didn't even make sense to begin with.

Taking another deep breath, I got to the bottom of the stairs and waited for a break in the action.

"Hey," I said after he had completed his move. I didn't want him to get killed by a zombie simply because I'd distracted him at the wrong time.

He paused the game and looked over, grinning. "Hey! About time."

"I can't stay," I said, walking over to the chair beside him, suddenly too nervous to even think about sitting on the couch next to him.

His smile faltered a little. "Oh. How come?"

"My dad's not home yet. We haven't even eaten dinner."

"Wow. That kind of stinks."

I nodded.

He glanced back at the TV and started up the game again. "You could have just texted me."

"I know. But I wanted to talk to you about something."

He paused the game and looked at me. "Sounds serious." He frowned. "Is something wrong?"

Yes. It's wrong that I'm sort of freaking out and feel like I don't know how to talk to you anymore. "No, no," I said, hoping I sounded more normal to him than I did in my head. "I just wanted to ask you . . . uh . . . are you going to the dance?"

He blinked a few times, his head sort of rolling back as though that was about the last thing he'd expected me to say. I might as well have just asked him about his next trip to Mars. "I wasn't planning on it. Why?"

"Uh, no," I said, waving off the idea and laughing. "Of course you wouldn't go. Um . . . so. What do you think of Olivia? She got really tall over the summer, huh?"

He did some more blinking and frowned. "Yeah. I guess."

"It makes her a really good dancer. Being so tall, I mean. Like a gazelle," I said. Because I couldn't seem to stop babbling. This was exactly why I hadn't come over since he'd returned from camp—ugh, could I be any lamer?

"Like a *what*?"

"A gazelle. You know, like an antelope? We learned about them in that unit on African savannahs? Oh, wait, you weren't at school last year, so maybe you don't know about savannahs. I have a book on them, if you want to borrow it. Really interesting stuff. Gazelles, I mean. And savannahs."

He scrunched up his nose. "Kat, is something wrong?"

Yes. I like you and I can't stop talking. "No, why?"

"Because you're acting weird, your face is red, and your voice is kind of . . . screechy."

"Is not!" I screeched.

Sigh. I tried again. "It's not. And I'm fine. I'm just wondering what you think of Olivia, that's all."

He shrugged and looked away. "I don't know. I've never really thought about it."

"Well, think!"

He turned his wide eyes back to me. "What?"

"Sorry," I said. "I meant, she's so beautiful, don't you think?"

"I guess so," he said, shrugging again. He turned back to the TV and started up the game. Not a good sign, but I pressed on.

"And she is sooooo popular this year already."

"So?" he asked as he stabbed a zombie in the eye with his broadsword.

"I don't know," I said. "I just thought you'd be into her."

"She's not really my type."

My heart lurched at that. He had a type? More than that, he'd *thought* about his type enough to know she wasn't it? "What's your type?"

He glanced at me for half a second and then back at the TV. "I don't know. Someone with a brain, I guess. Someone who doesn't obsess over which 'boy-band hottie' she wants to kiss most."

Uh-oh, time to do damage control. "When she did that speech in homeroom about her band boyfriend, she was doing it *ironically*," I said, hoping I was using the word right. "She didn't really mean it. She was being funny. She has a really good sense of humor."

He looked at me, and I knew he wasn't buying it.

"Anyway, she's definitely the girl you want to be with at the dance, if you know what I mean. . . ."

He paused the game again and looked at me. "What's going on here, Kat?"

I swallowed as a million thoughts whirled around

in my brain and I scrambled to sort out something to say. "Nothing, just, uh . . ."

Thanks a lot, brain.

"And I thought we were going to do a scavenger hunt this past weekend," he said, scrunching up his face into a frown. "I miss those."

I cringed and looked down at my hands. We used to do these goofy scavenger hunts where I'd climb up the tree that went right to his window and we'd exchange lists of ten items to gather—things like werewolf hair (which Hector "donated"), a hawk master's gauntlet (one of Mrs. Lot's rubber kitchen gloves), dragon's blood (hummingbird-feeder nectar), and even fairy dust (Laura was *not* happy when I made it out of one of her sparkly eye shadows). Whoever collected all the items first won. The prize was usually something dumb—like getting knighted or having the loser be the winner's servant for the day—but it never mattered. It was more about the game.

On Saturday, Tyler had texted me that he had a list ready for our first hunt of the school year, but I'd bailed, too nervous to spend that much time with him. Even though, at the same time, I really missed doing the hunts too. We always had so much fun and laughed like crazy at what we'd come up with for the items.

I just wanted things to get back to how they were. But how could that happen when I felt like barfing every time I was around him?

"I had to do a bunch of chores," I said, still not looking at him.

"Really?" he asked, and I could tell he didn't believe me.

I hated lying to him, but what could I say? *You're too cute now and I don't know how to be your friend anymore without it being weird?*

I nodded and changed the subject. "Anyway, I just thought you'd want to talk about Olivia. You don't know her all that well, but since you're at school with us now, you're going to be spending a lot more time with her."

"Not if I can help it," he muttered as he started up the game again.

Ugh. Not a good sign.

Before I could say anything to that, my phone buzzed in my pocket. "I've got to go," I said.

"See you tomorrow," he said as he stabbed another zombie in the heart.

Which was exactly what I was going to do to Olivia.

Chapter 4

I HAD HOPED TO EASE OLIVIA INTO THE WHOLE Tyler-isn't-into-you conversation, which means I was kind of chicken and hoped she'd forgotten about it. But the second she saw me in the hall the next morning, she used her superlong legs to glide up to me immediately.

"So? How did it go?" she asked. Her eyes were wide and hopeful, which just made me feel worse.

I stepped around her so I could get to my locker. "How did *what* go?" I asked as if I had no clue what she was talking about.

She didn't buy it and rolled her eyes. "With Tyler. About him asking me to the dance."

I didn't remember promising that *he* would actually ask *her* to the dance, but I knew bringing that up wasn't going to do any good. So I busied myself with opening my locker, trying to figure out how to tell her it wasn't going to work between her and Tyler.

"Kat?" she barked loudly, startling me enough that I almost banged my head into the locker.

I swiveled toward her. "What?"

She looked at me like I'd lost my marbles. "Hello? Tyler? Dance?"

Fighting the urge to sigh, I turned back to the locker so I wouldn't have to look into her eyes. I *really* didn't want to hurt her feelings but . . . "I just . . . I don't think he's the right guy for you."

"Why not?"

Not wanting to give away what he'd said, because I knew it would hurt her, I figured I'd focus on their differences. "Like I said, he's really into games and comics and stuff. He's kind of a nerd like that. He doesn't know all the words to every 5Style song or have their posters plastered all over his bedroom walls."

She was silent for so long that I had to turn and

look at her, scared I'd totally offended her. She was staring at me with a look on her face I couldn't figure out. I brought my thumb to my mouth and nibbled on my fingernail, waiting.

She blinked five times (yes, I counted) before she said, "He's a *really cute* nerd. And I don't care what music he listens to."

Ugh. So that hadn't worked. "He reads *a lot* and plays Xbox all the time he's not reading. I don't even know if he has time for, like, a girlfriend."

"I won't hold the reading and the gaming things against him," she assured me. Then she cocked her head to the side and narrowed her eyes. "Wait. Do you not want me to go to the dance with him?"

My mouth went dry as I thought about my answer. I shoved my hands in my pockets and had to clear my throat before I could speak. "It's not that, Livvy. I just . . . you two don't have anything in common."

"My parents have nothing in common, and they've been married almost twenty years."

Yes, but Tyler thinks you're only about makeup and boy bands.

I had nothing I could actually say to her, so I turned back to my locker, unloaded my lunch, and took out my books for first period.

She sighed. "What do I have to do to make him notice me? I did my best flirting yesterday at lunch, but he seemed more interested in your hard-boiled egg."

That should have been your first clue, I thought. "Are you sure you want *him*, Livvy?"

Honestly, with the way she looked and her being on the dance team, she could have *any* guy. Maybe even eighth-graders. "What about TJ Stevens or—"

"I don't care about TJ Stevens. I like *Tyler*," she said, cutting me off midsentence. I could tell by that determined look in her eye and the way her arms were crossed and her back was super straight that she wasn't going to let up. "He's cute and everyone likes him."

As I stood there and thought about how she was my cousin and friend and how much I really did love her, I realized maybe I sort of owed it to her to make it happen for her and Tyler. I mean, Tyler would never in a million years go for *me*, so why wouldn't I want him with my best cousin? Once he got to really know her, of course he'd change his mind about her. Right?

I closed my locker door and turned back toward her. "Fine. I am going to shelve books in the library at lunch today, but why don't you come over after school and we'll figure it out."

Before the words were even out of my mouth, Olivia was bouncing on her toes and clapping her hands. "Thank you so much, Kat!" she squealed.

"Okay, so this right here?" I said, gesturing toward her bouncing body. "It's going to have to go. You can't be all squealy and fangirly around him."

She stopped the bouncing, and her smile dissolved. "Oh. Right." But then she grinned at me and resumed the bouncing, although not quite as high. "But I can do it around *you*, can't I? Because I'm so excited I can't help it!"

I smiled at her. I kind of loved how enthusiastic she was sometimes, though I'd never admit that to her. "Yeah, sure, Livvy. You can bounce around me all you like."

But I couldn't help thinking that, boy, did I have a job ahead of me.

Chapter 5

TYLER HAD SAID HE WANTED A GIRL WITH A BRAIN. Someone who didn't obsess over boy bands. Those were two big things I was going to have to help Olivia with. I mean, she does have a brain; it's just normally occupied with things like . . . boy bands.

Sigh.

Realizing we would need more time, in gym I had asked if she wanted to stay for dinner. Dad was at some sort of seminar and wouldn't be home until late, so I knew we'd be eating at a reasonable hour because we wouldn't have to wait for him. Of course she'd said yes, and Mom had said it was okay when I texted her to ask, so that would give us a few hours to work on what I was calling Project Ty-Livia.

"So here's the thing," I said to her as I closed my bedroom door. Olivia plopped down on my bed, keeping a safe distance between herself and the sleeping Hector. "You're going to have to show him your inner nerd."

"*What* inner nerd?" she said, looking at me suspiciously.

I came over and sat on the bed, absently petting Hector. "The inner nerd who is interested in the kinds of things he likes. And like I said before, you can't do the over-the-top stuff. No squealing, no clapping, no hair tossing."

She frowned at me. "But what if I'm excited about something?"

I shook my head. "He doesn't like drama. Just be . . . you know, chill."

She seemed to think about that for a minute and then nodded. "Right, *chill*," she said in a calm, low voice.

"Yeah, like that," I said, glad she was catching on.

"You can start by talking to him about books. He's a big reader."

She scrunched up her nose.

"What?"

"You know I don't read. Not unless I have to for school."

I got up off the bed and stepped over to my bookshelf, grabbing my worn copy of *Knights at Sunrise*, the first of the Blackwood Knights series. I turned and held out the book toward her.

"What's that?" she asked, looking at it as though it were a snake or something. She made no movement to take it from me.

"Tyler's favorite book."

"It's huge."

I shrugged.

"There's a dragon on the cover."

"It's *about* dragons," I told her. "And knights, of course."

She looked from the book up to my eyes. "You expect me to read that? It has to be a thousand pages."

Actually, more like five hundred, but it wasn't

something I needed to point out. "Do you want Tyler to connect with you? He loves nothing more than talking about this book and the ones that come after."

"There are more?" she whined.

"Yes, seven more. But start with this one."

She huffed but took the book finally. "Can't you just tell me what it's about?"

"It's actually a really good book, Livvy. It's about these eight knights that meet as children and grow up to become . . ." I stopped talking when she stuck out her tongue and rolled her eyes so hard all I could see was the whites. I laughed. "Okay so you don't have to *love* the book, but at least give it a try. If you can talk to him about it, I guarantee he will be impressed."

She huffed again but nodded. "Fine. What else?"

"Are you willing to play video games?"

Her eyes lit up. "Like the ones where you dance?"

I couldn't imagine Tyler dancing *at all*, let alone in a video game. "Uh, no. I'm thinking more like Zombie Slashers."

Another eye roll. "Nope. Next?"

"Movies?"

She looked at me sideways. "What kind of movies?"

"Mostly ninja and samurai movies. Some of the comic-book ones. He watches a lot of anime, too."

"Like Disney movies?" she asked.

"No, not animated movies—*anime*," I said, trying not to be mean about it, but seriously, how did she not know what anime was? I was sure I'd talked about it a million times. "You know, the Japanese-style shows I watch sometimes?"

"The ones with the big eyes?"

"Yeah."

"Those are *animated*, Kat," she said as though *I* were the clueless one. *Whatever.*

"Anyway, that's what he watches."

She looked down at the book in her hand. "I guess I'll start with this. Any chance the movie version is on Netflix?"

"No." I shook my head. "There's *going* to be a movie, but it's in preproduction." I knew this from surfing the author's website the weekend after I finished the last book in the series for the third time. "We don't have time to wait for it, though."

"Awesome," she said, clearly not meaning it. "So tell me more about him so I can impress him. I guess all I really know is that he's good at math; he always seems to know all the answers in class."

I sat back down on the bed beside her, nodding. "He's *really* good at math. He wants to be either a mathematician or an architect when he grows up."

"Okay, that's cool," she said. Finally, something we could agree on! "What other things does he like?"

I thought about that. "Well, he likes animals." Though I didn't think that fact was going to help very much, since Olivia wasn't an animal lover. She didn't mind Hector so much, probably because all he did was lie there beside her. But she'd hated dogs ever since that Thanksgiving when we were four and our uncle Fred's giant Great Dane had barreled into her and knocked her down.

"What's his favorite food?"

"Hamburgers," I said, reaching over and giving Hector a scratch on the head. He yawned and got up to stretch before settling himself on my legs to continue his nap.

"That's weird, isn't it?" she asked.

I looked up at her. "What?"

"Hamburgers?"

I shrugged. "I don't know. It's what he likes. But he likes most food. Except olives."

"Hmm. I like olives," she said.

This is when you're supposed to realize you have nothing in common with him AT ALL *and change your mind about wanting to go to the dance with him.* Unfortunately, Olivia couldn't read my mind.

"So what else does he like to do? What did he do over the summer that made him so tan?"

I was about to tell her about his wilderness camp when there was a knock at my bedroom door. A half second later Laura opened it really quickly, like she was hoping to bust us doing something wrong. All she did was scare Hector half to death, making him jump off me, but not before he dug all of his claws into my legs.

"Laura!" I yelled. "Ugh! Ow!"

She rolled her eyes at me. "Whatever. Mom said to wash up and come set the table for dinner."

"Hi, Laura," Olivia said.

Laura grunted something but didn't even look at Olivia before she left. So rude! But my horrid sister wasn't my immediate concern. I was wearing jeans, so I couldn't see exactly what Hector had done to my legs, but the burning sensation told me I was going to have red welts all over.

"When did she get so mean? She wasn't like that at the Fourth of July barbecue," Olivia said.

I shrugged as I stood up. "I don't know. Mostly since starting high school a couple of weeks ago. I try to stay away from her."

"I don't blame you. You okay?" she asked as I cringed at the pain in my legs.

I did a quick check of my legs under my pants, and sure enough, there were puffy red scratches on both of them. At least they weren't bleeding.

Hector: Ninja Cat strikes! I was going to make a joke out of it, but outside of my family, only Tyler knew about my manga, and I wanted to keep it that way—for now, at least—so I kept my mouth shut.

"Holy cow!" Olivia said. "Your cat did that just now?"

"Yeah. But it was Laura's fault."

Olivia looked at me funny. "Uh, not to point out the obvious, but the *cat* did that to you, not your sister. Your sister is mean, for sure, but cats are evil. Ugh. I can't believe you even have a pet that could do that to you."

I tried to ignore the itchy and stinging scratches, knowing they would go away eventually. "He's normally very sweet."

"Right," she said, but I could tell she wasn't convinced.

"Come on," I said, heading toward the door. "We'd better go downstairs."

Chapter 6

THE NEXT DAY AT LUNCH, THE THREE OF US—
Olivia, Tyler, and me—were in the cafeteria. Laura had
assembled my lunch, which meant it wasn't as bad as
Dad's, but it wasn't exactly fine dining. She'd put one
shaved piece of turkey between two slices of bread (no
mustard!) and thrown it in a bag with a whole apple
(which of course I couldn't eat) and loose fish crack-
ers, which had crumbled into cracker dust under the
apple. I suppose I should have been happy it wasn't a
boiled egg and a can of sardines.

Anyway, there we were, eating and talking. Well,
Olivia was talking. Tyler was doing a lot of blinking

and staring. He was too polite to tell her he wasn't at all interested in her dance-team stuff, but it wasn't like he *looked* interested. She was totally clueless. I tried to catch her eye to make her stop, but she just went on and on, while we sat there staring at her. I was definitely going to have to talk to her about getting carried away and babbling when no one was listening, but there wasn't much I could do about it while Tyler was with us.

Finally, Tyler seemed to have had enough. "So what did you think of that math assignment we got today?" he asked us. He kind of cut Olivia off, but he hardly had a choice, since she never stopped to take a breath!

"Oh," she said, her face falling as she thought about math, her worst subject. "I don't know. It looks really hard."

Tyler is a math whiz, so I wasn't at all surprised when he said, "It's not that hard—you just have to work through the stuff we've learned already and apply it to the problems in the assignment."

She glanced at me as if to say, *Really?* but then turned back to him. "I'm not very good at math, but

I'm sure it's because of Ms. Carter; normally I'm really smart."

Tyler opened his mouth. I was sure he was going to defend our teacher, so I cut in before he could.

"Hey, Tyler, maybe you could help Olivia with the assignment," I suggested. "Since you're so good at math, and it actually is pretty hard for people who aren't *math geniuses*."

Tyler looked over at me, blushing a little. I normally loved teasing him about being so brainy, but his blush suddenly made me feel weird. Like panicky weird.

He didn't seem to notice, though. He cleared his throat and said, "Yeah, I guess I could do that. Should we go to the library after school?"

Olivia gave him her brightest smile. "Oh, that would be perfect! Thank you so much!"

"So what do you say? We'll meet in the library right after last class?" Tyler asked, looking at me.

I glanced at Olivia, who must have realized that Tyler was expecting *all three of us* to go to the library. She gave me a tiny panicked shake of her head. Right: She wanted to be alone with him.

"Er . . . I can't. I have to . . ." I couldn't think of anything as they both looked at me. I had to come up with *something*!

"Don't you have to make dinner tonight for your family?" Olivia said helpfully.

Thank you, Olivia! "Yes! That's right. I promised my mom I would help with dinner tonight," I said way too loudly. The kid at the table next to us actually stopped midchew to stare.

Tyler narrowed his eyes at me. "You okay, Kat?"

"Of course!" I realized that my really eager voice probably wasn't all that convincing, so I toned it down. "Of course. Just really excited about tonight's dinner!"

He smiled back at me. "I didn't know you were into cooking. What are you making?"

I stared at him for a second and then glanced over at Olivia for help. She thankfully clued in and said, "She's making lasagna. Since it takes so long to make, she has to go right home *the second* school ends."

"Yeah," I said. "Right away, so I can't go to the library at all. But you two go. I'm sure you'll get that assignment worked out, Olivia."

"I'm sure I will too," she said, making googly eyes at Tyler.

Too bad he didn't notice; he was busy looking at his phone.

I probably should have gone home after school, especially since I knew my mom actually would have appreciated some help with dinner, but I was too curious about Tyler and Olivia's study session. So I said good-bye to the two of them at our lockers and pretended I needed to use the bathroom on my way out of school, giving them a few minutes to get settled in the library before I could follow and spy on them.

Two seconds after I entered the restroom, though, the door burst open and a panicked Olivia practically bashed into me.

"Wha?" I managed to say, grabbing onto her arms to steady her. "What's going on?"

"Oh, Kat. I'm so glad you came in here!" she panted. "He *still* doesn't seem to get when I'm flirting with him. Like, at lunch I gave him my best looks and talked about dance, but I don't think it's working! Will you give me some pointers before I go to the library with him?"

I looked at her sideways. "Pointers? What do you mean?"

"You know, like what I should say, stuff like that."

Right, because I was some sort of pro at flirting or something. "I don't know. Talk about the book. You did read some of it, right?"

She nodded. "Yep, I did. Okay, great. What else?"

"Uh . . ." I thought for a second. "What do you know about football?"

"Less than nothing!" she said, and then her eyes filled up and her lip quivered.

Oh no. I grabbed her arm and squeezed encouragingly. "Livvy, it's okay. Chill out. Just talk about the book. Get him started and he'll take it from there. He can seriously talk about those books for *hours*. And if that doesn't work, you may as well get him to help you with the assignment—you know, the reason you're meeting with him in the first place?"

She nodded, and even though she still looked pretty frazzled, she seemed like she wasn't about to have a meltdown anymore. Whew. Crisis averted.

"You'd better get out there."

She nodded again and then threw her arms around me. "Thank you so much, Kat. You're the *best* best cousin ever."

I squeezed her and let her go. "Go on. Text me later."

She agreed she would and then left the bathroom.

It's not wrong to peek in on your friends, I told myself as I watched her go. And anyway, I wasn't going to stay long; I just wanted to see what happened. Something told me it was going to be a disaster, which made my heart ache for Olivia. Deep down, I didn't *really* want her to get hurt, but she seemed so sure Tyler was the guy for her. This couldn't end well, but secretly I didn't want to miss it, even though I knew it made me a horrible friend and cousin.

I waited as long as I could in the bathroom and then snuck out into the hall, relieved that it was mostly empty. I walked to the library, hoping they weren't near the door. Knowing Olivia, she would have done her best to get him back into the quieter area, where there were some tables behind a bunch of stacks.

"I wasn't expecting you this afternoon," a voice came from beside me as I passed the checkout desk. It scared me almost out of my skin.

After I managed to not scream in terror, I turned and saw the librarian, Ms. Watkins, who was smiling at me. I helped her reshelve books a few times a week, but usually during a free period or lunch.

"Oh, uh, no," I said. "I'm just here looking around for a bit. My dad works late these days, so there's no rush to get home."

"I'm here for another half hour or so," she said, waving toward the stacks. "You know where everything is."

Well, not *everything*, I didn't say, turning to scan the library for my friends. Sure enough, I didn't see them immediately, which meant I was going to have to sneak around the stacks.

Or . . . I had an idea. I turned back toward Ms. Watkins. "Can I go into a music room?"

Without a word she reached into her desk, grabbed a big wooden key chain in the shape of a number two, and held it out toward me. "Bring it back in thirty minutes so I don't have to come searching for you."

"Thanks," I said, taking the key. This was perfect: The music rooms were up on the second floor of the library and overlooked the back section where all the tables were, so I'd be able to spy on them and they'd never know I was even there. I wouldn't be able to hear what they were saying, but you can tell a lot by body language. Like when my mom crosses her arms and Dad pinches the bridge of his nose: Those things mean Laura is driving them crazy.

I took the stairs up to the mezzanine and went along the hall to music room two, unlocking the door and then stepping inside and up to the window, where I peeked through the mostly closed blinds.

Aha! There they were, down on the main floor, sitting at a round table next to each other.

Olivia was talking. Surprise surprise.

Tyler pointed at her backpack and said something, probably something like, "Let's get this over with so I can get home and play Zombie Slashers."

Olivia smiled at him and then said something else

as she reached for her backpack. Maybe: "Oh, right. Ha-ha, let me get my book out and you can help me ace this assignment. Also, I really want you to take me to the Fall Ball because you're so cute this year. I love your mysterious hair!"

Okay, she probably didn't say most of that—especially that last part—but she was likely thinking it. She sure was doing a lot of talking. She slid her notebook out of her bag as she talked. Then she talked some more as she flipped the book open and found the right page. I knew she always talked a lot, but with him just sitting there, it was really obvious just how much.

I looked from her to Tyler; he was frowning. Then he said a few words. She said something else, and he frowned more.

Then, all of a sudden, she got up out of her chair and started jumping around.

"What are you doing?" I whispered, even though she couldn't possibly hear me.

Wait . . . could she be . . . ? Yes! She was dancing in the middle of the library!

No! I glanced over at him, and he was all wide-eyed as he stared at her, and I could only imagine what was going through his head. That she was completely crazy, I guessed.

It was pretty much the worst thing she could have done. I had to help her. But how?

Before I got the chance to come up with anything, Tyler said something and rose from the table. He didn't gather his things, so at least he wasn't bailing on her, but he walked quickly toward the bathrooms. The second he rounded the corner out of sight, Olivia grabbed her phone out of her pocket, and seconds later mine rang.

I was going to ask her what on earth she was doing, but I quickly remembered I wasn't supposed to be in the school, let alone spying on her, so instead I took a breath and answered normally.

Not that she would have noticed, since I barely got out my hello before she screeched: "Kat!"

I had to hold the phone away from my face. "Livvy? What's going on?"

"It's going sooooo wrong! Kat, it's a complete disaster. You have to help me!"

"What do you mean?" I asked, even though I already knew it wasn't going well.

"Well, I started talking about that Blackburn Knights book—"

"It's Black*wood* Knights," I corrected her.

"Whatever! Anyway," she said, "I told him I was reading it and loved the part about that guy Kincaid and how he won the duel and then the part when the dragons went into the rainbows and—"

"Livvy," I said, cutting her off again. "You got a few facts wrong. His name is Kin*cairn*. And he *lost* the duel when he was almost killed by his brother, who tried to murder him to become heir to the throne. And the dragons didn't go into *rainbows*; they were all killed at the Battle of Reignbough. Did you actually read the book?"

"Uh . . . yeah, I did . . . sort of. I mean, I was watching *The Bachelor* at the same time, but I flipped through some of the pages."

I sighed. "Livvy. You need to know what you're talking about; you can't just skim and then fill in the rest with stuff you make up. He's smart and will catch on."

"But it was *so boring*," she whined. "Why can't you just tell me what happens in the book? I wish you could be in my head and help me do this."

"Yeah, well, I can't," I said absently. I looked at my phone's screen because a text had come in.

Tyler: *Olivia is nuts!*

Uh-oh.

Kat: *No. Just bad at math.*

Tyler: *she was just dancing.*

At least he recognized it as dancing.

Kat: *she's a great dancer! Where r u?*

Tyler: *Bathroom. But why is she dancing?*

Kat: *maybe she's nervous*

"Kat! Are you there?" Livvy squealed through the phone, reminding me I was still talking to her. "I asked you what you think!"

"Sorry. My mom was talking to me. What I think about what?"

She sighed loudly. "Helping me."

"I *am* helping you."

"No, I mean helping me figure out what to say to him."

"How?"

There was a short pause. "I'll put my earbuds in and hide them in my hair, and you can just tell me what to say."

"But how will I know what he's saying?" I asked.

"My microphone! My hair doesn't cover it totally, but it sort of blends in, so I don't think he'll see. You'll be able to hear enough."

My stomach rolled over at the thought of doing that. It felt wrong to dupe Tyler that way: It was one thing to coach her on how to impress him, but this felt kind of dishonest. "I don't know, Livvy."

"Please, Kat. I need your help. I can't do this on my own."

I looked out the window down to where she was now sitting at the table and saw her wipe her eyes. Ugh. She was starting to cry. If Tyler came back from the bathroom and saw her crying, he was really going to think she was bonkers.

Speaking of him, another text came in.

Tyler: *what would she be nervous about?*

How cute you are? How she wants to go to the

dance with you and you're not taking the hint?

Kat: *maybe you thinking she's not smart.*

Tyler: *She's not dumb, she's WEIRD.*

Kat: *she's trying to make you laugh, I bet. She's very funny.*

Tyler: *ok, better get back.*

"Livvy?" I said into the phone. "He's coming back."

"He is?" she said, looking around. And then she added, "How do you know?"

Oops.

"I mean, I assume he is. How long can a guy spend in the bathroom?"

"Right. Okay, hold on," she said, and I watched as she fiddled with her earbuds and pulled her long hair forward. She slipped the phone into her back pocket behind her. "Can you hear me?" she asked.

"Yeah," I said.

"Okay, shhhh," she said. "He's coming back."

Duh, Livvy, he can't hear me, I thought but didn't say.

Tyler sat down across from her, and even from where I was, I could see that things were weird between them; they were both very stiff and had pinched looks on their faces.

"So," Olivia said while I was still trying to figure out how to fix what she'd messed up. "How was the bathroom? Anything new in there?"

What? Ugh, Livvy, I thought. Tyler just stared at her, and I seriously wondered if he was going to get up and leave.

But even Olivia seemed to figure out how lame she was being, because she cringed and blurted out, "I mean, not that I need to know how it was— just . . . uh . . . making sure you . . ." She trailed off, and her face got really red. "So all those dragons got killed, huh?"

I exhaled in relief. Okay, so I could help her from here, now that she'd gone back to talking about *Knights at Sunrise.*

Tyler wasn't on board yet, though. "What?"

I whispered into my phone. "Tell him you just read the part about the battle at Reignbough where the dragons were all slain by Glengarry. Tell him you didn't see it coming when Glengarry found Diana."

"Okay, right," she said, answering me before she

turned to Tyler. *Jeez, Livvy.* I shook my head. "So I just couldn't believe that Glengarry killed all the dragons at Reignbough!"

Tyler frowned. "But you said before that—"

She waved a hand at him and smiled. "I was joking before. Of course I know the dragons didn't really go into the rainbows."

"Tell him that was a metaphor for them dying," I said into the phone, sort of proud of myself for coming up with something so clever.

"I mean," she said, making her face very serious, "them dying was very sad, but they went up to heaven. Like they flew through the rainbows to *get* to heaven. That's what I meant before."

"Oh," Tyler said, nodding and half smiling. "Yeah, sort of."

"But then," Olivia said, leaning over the table and making her eyes wide, "when Glengarry got together with Diana—I totally did not see that ship coming. But they make such a great couple!"

"No!" I hissed loudly into the phone, unable to stop myself. "Diana is the magic bow of the huntress!

That's what Glengarry used to slay the dragons—it's not a girl! It's a weapon!"

I looked down at them and watched as all the color drained from her face. I felt so bad—maybe I should have been more specific about Diana being a bow, but she'd said she'd read the book, and if she'd just stayed on script . . .

"It's okay, it's okay," I said quickly into the phone. "Just tell him that every great warrior needs a powerful weapon and that of course Diana was his, and the way the bow fit into his hands, it was almost like a relationship." It was a stretch, but . . .

She laughed, although it sounded pretty fake. "I'm kidding. Ha-ha! I mean, of course Diana is a bow, but—"

"You're right, though," Tyler said, leaning over the table, suddenly looking excited. "After Imogen was kidnapped by Kendrake, Glengarry said he felt like he'd lost a part of himself, and when he found Diana in the cave, he said he felt strangely whole again. I love that you picked up on that. I've read the book so many times, but I never really looked at it that way. Wow,

Olivia." And then he smiled at her while he pushed his hair back off his forehead.

Then the strangest feeling came over me. As I stared down at the two of them, I suddenly felt a little . . . mad. And sad at being left out.

Then Tyler said, "I wish Kat was here; she loves talking about this stuff. I bet she'd love your take on Glengarry finding Diana too."

"No I wouldn't," I muttered.

"No she wouldn't," Olivia repeated, as though I'd meant for her to. Tyler tilted his head and looked at her, but she didn't seem to understand the funny expression on his face.

"Anyway," she said. "Kat's *not* here. It's just you and me."

"Right," I said drily.

Olivia cleared her throat. "Like I said, *just* you and me."

"I'm going to hang up, Livvy," I said, suddenly not wanting to be involved in this anymore.

"You can't!" she said. Tyler must have given her a weird look, because then she started to stutter. "I-I mean . . . you can't be done telling me about all the stuff you're into. What's the last movie you saw?"

Tyler started talking about these new samurai movies he'd just gotten on DVD—ones that I actually hadn't seen—and when I told Olivia in her ear that I couldn't help her, she managed to get Tyler to offer to lend them to her.

Something in my heart twisted at that; he hadn't even offered them to *me* yet.

I whispered in Olivia's ear that I needed to go help my mom with the rest of dinner (mostly because I wanted to return the key back to Ms. Watkins before she came looking for me and blew my cover), so she told him she had to go home. I heard him say that they hadn't even worked on the math assignment yet and that maybe they should get together again tomorrow after school too. He didn't even sound upset about it.

That's when I knew that the plan was working even better than either she or I could have hoped.

We were doing it: We were getting Tyler to like her. Project Ty-Livia was well on its way.

Awesome.

Chapter 7

I WASN'T EVEN HALFWAY HOME WHEN OLIVIA texted me to let me know she was leaving the school and asked if she could come over. I panicked, worried that her gazellelike legs would help her catch up with me and she'd figure out I hadn't gone straight home from school. So I told her I was busy, but if she wanted to come over after dinner, that would be okay.

Luckily, Dad wasn't too late that night, so by the time Olivia knocked on the door, we were done eating. I'd just closed the dishwasher after loading it.

I could tell by the way she was acting all jittery

that she had news for me. I led her up to my bedroom and closed the door, but before I could even turn back around, Olivia had thrown her arms around me.

"Thank you so much!" she said, squeezing me so tight I was worried she was squashing my organs.

"Urgle . . . ," I muttered. "Let me go, Livvy."

She did, so suddenly I almost fell over. "Oh, right! Sorry." She grinned at me, bouncing on her toes. "I'm just so excited. It went really well, and we're meeting again tomorrow!"

"I heard." I smiled at her because I couldn't help it. She was obviously really happy, and her excitement was contagious.

"And don't worry: You won't have to help as much as you did today. I really do need help with that math assignment, so we can talk about that and then maybe he'll ask me to the dance."

Wait. What? "What do you mean I won't have to help *as much*?"

She looked at me like I wasn't speaking English. "Well. Because we won't be talking about all that boring stuff, like the books and the movies."

"Right," I said. "The boring stuff." All the stuff Tyler likes. All the stuff *I* like.

"But you're going to have to still be on the phone with me. Obviously," she said with a smile. Like maybe I *wanted* to do all this.

"Livvy . . . I don't think so."

Her face fell, and her eyes filled with tears. "But . . . but . . . what if he *wants* to talk about that stuff?"

I sighed. "Fine. But you have to promise to read the books and watch the movies; he's going to figure it out after a while if you don't." Plus, I didn't want to be stuck doing this forever.

"Of course," she said. "I'll read the boring books and watch the dumb movies this weekend. I just need your help tomorrow. I was so nervous he was going to want to keep talking about that stuff that I made my mom pick me up from school instead of letting him walk me home, which would have been way better. But I couldn't risk it, you know? I wish there was a quick way to learn all these things! It's going to take so long. . . ." She frowned and looked up at the ceiling, which I knew meant she was thinking. "Unless . . ."

"What?" I asked, suddenly suspicious.

"Maybe you can make me a list of everything."

"Everything?"

Her eyes lit up. "Yeah, you know, all the stuff about the books and movies and what he likes and doesn't like."

"But I told you all that stuff. About *Knights at Sunrise* and Zombie Slashers and that his favorite food is hamburgers and—"

"Hamburgers?" Olivia said. "I thought you said tacos."

"No. I would never say tacos, Livvy."

"See?" she said, her eyes getting glassy again. "This is why I need your help!"

Without another word I grabbed a notebook out of my backpack and ripped out a blank page.

"But make it small," Olivia said. "So I can put it in my purse."

I stared at my cousin, biting my tongue because I was starting to feel a little crabby at everything she was making me do. I didn't want to help her with all this stuff. I mean, if she couldn't even remember details about him—important details—why should she get to go to the dance with him? I knew *everything* about him! Then again, that didn't matter, because he'd never like me that way.

She must have heard my angry thoughts, because she smiled at me and said, very sweetly, "Please."

I sighed. As much as I wanted to say no, I could tell that this really meant a lot to her. Plus, I was doing it for *both* my best friends, right? And kind of for me, too, because if I got them together, Tyler and I could go back to how we were before the summer, when things were easy and normal. It was a good plan for them to be together; they just needed (a lot of) help to make it happen.

Just then I had an idea.

"Wait here," I said, leaving my room and heading down the hall to Laura's. I knew I'd get in trouble for rooting around for something in her room, but I *really* hoped she wasn't there, because she'd been extra snotty at dinner and I totally wasn't in the mood. As soon as I knocked, I realized I wasn't that lucky.

"What?" she barked.

"Can I come in?"

She let out a huge sigh before she said I could.

"What is it? I'm doing homework," she said.

She was sitting at her desk in front of her computer with a bunch of words on the screen. Maybe she actually was doing homework—she hadn't played any video games since starting ninth grade this year, but I'd assumed that was because she was too busy with her new high school friends. Maybe school was more important for her this year. I wasn't about to ask, especially since I was there for a reason and needed to get back to Olivia. Not that Laura ever wanted to talk to me anyway.

"Do you have any of those little cards?" I asked.

She made an eye-rolly face. "What little cards?"

"The ones you used last year for your speech. Remember?"

"Index cards?"

That's it! Index cards. I nodded.

Her eyes narrowed at me. "Why?"

Ugh. What did she even care? "Laura, I just need them, okay? Can I just have some, please?"

"I'll give them to you if you tell me what they're for."

If I'd been smart and my sister hadn't been completely staring me down, I would have just said it was for school, but instead I stumbled over my words and said, "For something I'm doing with Olivia."

She swiveled back and forth on her desk chair, making it squeak annoyingly. She was someone who thought *everything* was annoying these days, but somehow that didn't seem to bother her.

"What kind of something?"

I was tired of all her questions, so I just broke down and told her the truth. "She likes Tyler and I'm writing down things about him for her."

Laura screwed up her face again. "Like cheat sheets about him?"

I shrugged. "I guess."

"She's not exactly his type, is she?"

I shrugged again. I wasn't going to say anything bad about her. "Can I have the cards now?"

Laura rolled her eyes and then swiveled her chair all the way around so she could pull open her bottom desk drawer. She dug around for a bit and then pulled out a stack of cards secured with a rubber band. She held them out toward me, so I stepped deeper into her room to take them.

But when I reached for them, she didn't let go. I looked into her eyes.

"Look," she said. "She's my cousin too, and of course I love her, but them together doesn't make a lot of sense. Anyway, I always thought *you* had a crush on him."

I felt my face get hotter than the sun. "What? No! Of course I don't," I said automatically, tugging on the cards, but she wasn't letting them go. "Can I have them, please?"

She looked at me sideways. "Are you sure you don't have a crush on him?"

"I'm sure. Give me the cards, Laura!"

"Why is your face so red?"

"It is not! Give. Me. The. Cards!"

Her eyebrows went up as she kept staring at me. I was just about to let go of the cards and run out of her room when she finally took her fingers away and swiveled away from me, back toward her computer.

"Fine. Fool yourself but you don't fool me."

Without another word I left her room. But I had to stop at the bathroom to calm down before I could face Olivia again.

By the time we were done, I'd filled six of the cards—both front *and* back—with every single detail about Tyler: his favorite foods and drinks, his favorite sports teams, video games, color, season, and anything else I could possibly think of. Also on the cards were details about *Knights at Sunrise* (even though she promised she would read the book), Zombie Slashers, anime, and other random things he liked.

"You sure do know a lot about him," she said as she tucked the cards into her purse.

I shrugged. "I know just as much about you."

"No you don't," she said. She didn't sound mad or anything. Maybe she was right that I knew more about him, which was weird because she and I are cousins. And best friends. Best cousins.

"I've known him practically my whole life. He's almost like . . ."

"A brother?"

No. Definitely not a brother. "Maybe," I said. Because I couldn't explain to her why he wasn't like a brother.

I thought she was going to call me on it anyway, but she happened to glance at the clock, and jumped up when she realized what time it was. "Uh-oh, my mom is probably downstairs in the car waiting for me. I'd better go. I'll see you at school tomorrow." She gave me a quick hug before we left my room, and I walked her to the door.

Chapter 8

AFTER ANOTHER EPISODE OF KAT THE PUPPET Master, where I spoke into Olivia's phone so she could impress Tyler with her (my) knowledge of all the things she (I) was into, I'd had about enough of Project Ty-Livia. In fact I was kind of tired of Olivia altogether, but we'd made plans for her to sleep over at my place that Friday because my aunt and uncle were going away for the night for their anniversary. So, after she rushed home after school to get her stuff, she showed up at my door.

I let her in and led her into the kitchen for a snack, since there was no telling when Dad would get home for us to eat. But as we were rooting through the fridge, Mom came in and took pity on us.

"Why don't we just order pizza tonight?" she asked.

"Really?" Mom almost never let us order pizza, even though it was my favorite.

"Sure," she said, nodding. "That okay with you, Livvy?"

"That would be great. Thanks, Aunt Judy," she said.

I grabbed the pizza-place menu out of the cupboard and brought it over to the island, opening it up so we could decide what to get. After some minor arguing (I wanted pineapple; Olivia declared pineapple was a crime against pizza), we left Mom to order and went to the den to wait for it to be delivered.

"So, I brought my makeup. Want to do makeovers?" Olivia asked as she dropped down onto the couch.

Olivia had never been into makeup before, but suddenly, now that we were in seventh grade, she was all about her appearance. As far as I was concerned, makeup was only good for making fairy dust for a scavenger hunt. It sure couldn't change a warthog into a gazelle.

I shook my head. "I was thinking I could show you Zombie Slashers and teach you how to play."

"Gaming?" She made a face. "Really? Can't we just find something on Netflix like we usually do?"

I ignored the face and went over to grab the two controllers, handing her one as I sat down beside her. "No. And yes, really. This is Tyler's favorite game."

"Okay. So it's about . . ." She looked at me and raised her eyebrows, waiting.

Seriously? "Slashing Zombies." *I mean, it's right there in the name.*

She sighed. "What do I do?"

"Let's start by making your character," I said.

Thirty minutes later we'd only just put the finishing touches on her pink-armored, blond, but very kick-butt character, when the doorbell rang: pizza.

"We'll come back after dinner," I said, putting down my controller and getting up.

"That was fun!" Olivia said, a big smile on her face.

"All we did was make your character."

"I know! I love that I got to choose what she looks like and wears and everything. It's so cool that you can make your character just like you, you know? I'm going to really like Zombie Slashers!"

I wasn't so sure, but at least she got the name right this time.

"I HATE Zombie Slashers!" Olivia announced only five minutes into the game. I had her on the easiest level, and she *still* couldn't seem to get the hang of even just moving her person around the training arena, let alone getting to where she could start fighting. Maybe this hadn't been such a great idea. I was just about to turn it off when a tall knight with a giant broadsword came up beside us.

Uh-oh.

"Who is that?" Olivia asked. "He doesn't look like a zombie. Or is it a trick?"

Shaking my head, I paused the game and reached for a headset, flipping the switch to turn it on and sliding it into place, adjusting it over my ear. "Hi, Ty," I said into the mic as I looked at Olivia and watched as she clued in, her eyes going wide.

She pointed at my mic and then at the screen, a

question on her face as though she had said out loud, *Is that really him?*

I nodded.

"You ready to get your butt kicked?" Tyler asked through the headset, and I could tell from his voice that he was smiling.

I couldn't help but smile back. "As if that's going to happen," I taunted, eager to show him my new moves. I'd been avoiding playing with him since he'd returned from camp, but playing with him this way—from different locations, so I didn't have to be all nervous sitting next to him—felt really good. Maybe I could do this. Maybe I could get over my nerves and get back to how we had been.

"Uh, Kat?" Olivia whispered, suddenly reminding me she was there. I passed her my sister's headset, knowing Laura wouldn't mind since she almost never played games anymore, and turned it on.

"Right. Yeah. So Olivia's here, too."

"Oh," Tyler said. "Hi, Olivia."

"Hi, Tyler," she said back in her sweet voice. "This is so fun!"

"So you play Zombie Slashers a lot?" he asked, sounding doubtful.

Not hardly, I didn't say out loud.

"All the time!" Olivia said.

What? "All the time"? I stared at her, and she smiled back at me like it was no big deal.

"Especially this past summer," she said. "I've been playing a lot in between dance-team practices."

"Hold on, Ty," I said. "My mom needs something."

I muted my headset and then reached over and did the same to Olivia's before I said, "What are you doing?"

She shrugged. "You said we should have more in common and that I should know about stuff he likes."

"Knowing about," I said, "is not the same as play-ing *all the time*. You haven't even played once!"

She put her controller in my hands. "Then you're going to have to play for me."

I looked down at the controller and then back up at her. "What?"

"Pretend you're me and play with him."

"I don't think so."

"And be good. I want him to be really impressed," she said like she hadn't heard me. Or had chosen not to.

"Livvy . . ."

"Kat. Please! *Dancing* is what I'm good at, not video games. I really like him a lot and I want him to like me, too. Please won't you help me with this? It's just a video game; it's not like you're cheating on a test or something."

I thought about that. She was right. But it still sort of felt like cheating. "Fine," I said.

She picked up my controller. "What are you doing?" I asked.

"I'm going to play as you."

I laughed at that. "Sorry, Livvy, but he won't believe I've gotten *that* bad over the summer. No offense."

She frowned but then nodded. "I guess you're right. What am I supposed to do, then?"

"Just watch and learn," I said, and then unmuted my headset.

She nodded and leaned toward me so I could unmute hers, too.

"Sorry, Ty," I said. "You there?"

"Yeah. What's up?"

"Oh, nothing. Mom just came to get the plates from our pizza."

"Pineapple and mushroom?" he asked.

"Of course!" I said, glancing over at Olivia. "At least on my half."

"That's the best," Tyler said.

Olivia made a face, making me laugh. I stuck my tongue out at her and then unpaused the game and moved her character over beside Tyler's.

"Let's play!" Tyler said. "Come on, Kat. Catch up with us."

"Oh, uh . . . ," I said, looking at Olivia because I hadn't worked out why "I" wasn't going to be playing.

"She shut her thumb in the door," Olivia said before I could even think of anything. "So she's just going to watch us play."

"Oh, but I can see you on the screen . . ."

"I was trying," I said. "But it hurts too much. You two go ahead."

"Okay," Tyler said. "Let's annihilate some zombies!"

"Yeah!" she said, clapping her hands, which I

guess didn't matter, since I was the one with hands on her controller.

After about an hour of zombie annihilating, I was thirsty and my hands were legitimately getting tired. I did a quick mute of my headset. "I need a break," I told Olivia quietly so Tyler wouldn't hear me through her microphone

She nodded. "Tyler, we're going to take a break to get some snacks."

"Why don't you come over and play here? I've got cheese popcorn, and my mom just made some brownies."

Playing with him over the past hour had finally felt just like old times—precrush times—even though I was pretending to be Olivia. Getting into our old routine of hunting down and killing (or rekilling) the zombies felt good, so the thought of going over there, sitting with him, and continuing the game sounded good to me. Not to mention, Mrs. Lot's brownies were awesome.

But going over there was obviously impossible if we were going to keep up our story.

"Thanks, but we're already in our pj's," I said.

"Okay," he said. "And, um, hey, maybe tomorrow you guys can come over?" He made it like a question. Like he really wanted us—both of us—to come over.

"That would be great!" Livvy said at the same time as I said, "We're busy."

I looked at her, because how could that happen? She smiled and shrugged at me.

"We're going to the mall tomorrow," I said, because it was the only thing I could think of.

"Right!" Olivia said. "To look at dresses for the upcoming Fall Ball." She said the words slowly like she really wanted him to pay attention to her talking about the dance.

"Oh, right. . . . Uh . . ."

I wondered if he was thinking about asking her to the dance. She and I exchanged looks, and I could tell she was thinking the same thing. My heart sped up as we waited for him to go on.

But instead of asking her, all he said was, "I'm glad we got to play together tonight, Livvy." It was weird hearing him use the nickname for her. He'd never used it before tonight.

"Me too," she said.

"You're even better at Zombie Slashers than Kat is!"

Olivia laughed at that, and I rolled my eyes. "Thanks a lot," I said.

"Sorry, Kat!" he said quickly, obviously not meaning to insult me. It was pretty funny, since he was telling me I was better than myself. Deep down, though, it did kind of hurt that he thought Olivia was so good when it was really me. Secretly, I wanted him to know I'd gotten so much better at the game over the summer, but now all he knew was that *Olivia* was really good. Better than me.

"It's okay," I said. "So is your mom going to drive us to the shelter on Sunday?"

"Oh yeah. I'll ask her, but I think so. Hey, Livvy, why don't you come with us? You can volunteer too."

Olivia looked at me. "Uh, maybe. I mean, I do love animals, obviously."

I fought the sigh that wanted to come out of my mouth so badly because she so did not love animals.

"Don't you have dance practice?" I asked her.

"No. You know I only have dance team on—"

"Okay, we'll talk about it," I said, interrupting her. "But she'd have to apply to be a volunteer. Anyway, we have to go right now. Bye!" I turned off the game then, even though Olivia had her mouth open to say something else.

"Hey!" she said to me. "We weren't done talking."

"Sorry," I said to her. "I thought you were. And since when do you love animals?"

She crossed her arms. "Since your animal-loving next-door neighbor got so cute."

I rolled my eyes. "One thing has nothing to do with the other."

"It does if it means I get to spend Sundays with him."

Taking the headset off, I got up off the couch and put the gaming stuff away. "Let's go see if there are any cookies."

Of course, what I really wanted were some of Mrs. Lot's amazing brownies, but that obviously wasn't happening, since I couldn't go next door.

At this rate it felt like I'd never get to go over there again.

Chapter 9

WE DID GO OVER TO TYLER'S LATER THAT evening—but only for a few minutes. Well, we didn't actually go *inside*; we just spoke through his kitchen window on the first floor after it took like twenty minutes for him to notice Olivia walking back and forth past the window. She stood there in the grass, explaining that she needed some fresh air after all the gaming, while I hid in the bushes in case he asked her anything about Zombie Slashers or *Knights at Sunrise*. I'd only agreed to do it if she got him to give up some of Mrs. Lot's brownies (yes, they are *that* good). And because she wouldn't stop babbling about going over there and I just wanted her to shut up.

On Saturday Tyler texted me to let me know his mom would be driving us to the animal shelter on Sunday. He said to come over at about nine thirty and reminded me to not forget my lunch. It was one of my dad's two Sundays a month volunteering there, doing surgeries and giving animals check-ups before they got adopted, but he would be starting early in the morning and Tyler and I weren't supposed to start our volunteer shift until ten. He would drive us home at the end of the day.

When I got to Tyler's on Sunday morning, we had to wait for his mom to finish getting ready, but it was a beautiful fall day, with the sky clear and blue, so we sat on the front porch stairs. He asked if Olivia would be meeting us at the shelter. I reminded him that we'd had to apply to the junior volunteer program and that she couldn't just show up. I really didn't think she'd actually be into it and hoped she'd forget she'd told him she thought it would be fun. Plus, okay, so maybe part of me didn't want her there.

"Oh yeah," he said—and was I imagining it, or did

his shoulders fall a little? "Well, I thought maybe she'd come to apply."

"*I'm* here, though," I said, a little hurt that he seemed to forget that *I* was his best friend and *we'd* planned to do this shelter thing together. *Us.* Tyler and Kat, not Tyler, *Olivia,* and Kat.

He smiled at me and leaned in to my shoulder. "Yeah. Sorry, Kat. I just . . . she's not what I thought, you know?"

I swallowed and said, "What do you mean?"

He shrugged. "You know what I thought of her before, but she's been . . . cool these last few days. I mean, she's into Zombie Slashers and has been reading *Knights at Sunrise* and everything. I mean, check out this text she sent me last night . . ." He showed me his phone.

Olivia: *I'm at the part in Nights at Sunrise where Kincairn is going to look for the gold chalice! So exciting.*

Tyler: *You're going to love the next part. Text me when you get there.*

Olivia: *I will! But tell me what happens next—I hate surprises!*

Tyler: *ha ha, I don't want to ruin it for you!*

Olivia: *no it's okay if you do. I like spoilers!*

He seemed to be enjoying texting with her. I shouldn't have been surprised. Although I had to admit it was kind of funny how she was trying to get him to tell her what happened in the book and how he wouldn't. I'm sure she didn't think it was quite as funny, though.

If only Tyler knew I'd made up a bunch of messages for her to use. Every word of the first text he showed me was mine. Except where she spelled "Knights" wrong—that was all her.

"Yeah, cool," I said.

He smiled at me. "And you were right—she really is funny. Sometimes she'll be talking about *Knights at Sunrise* and she'll pretend like she has no idea what's going on in the book. Like this one time"—he started giggling, and then it turned into a real laugh and I had to wait for him to finish—"she was talking about the dragons flying into the rainbows to heaven and them landing in the leprechauns' pots of gold or something. Like *rainbows*, not *Reignbough*. It was hilarious."

Poor Tyler had no clue. "See? I told you she's funny," I said, *not* adding *even when she doesn't mean to be.* I guess I should have been happy that our plan was working, except that instead of getting my mind off my crush on him, this whole thing was kind of just making me mad.

"Anyway, thanks," he said, bumping my shoulder again.

I looked over at him, hating the butterflies that took off in my belly just because of the little piece of hair that fell over his forehead. I mean, it's just hair!

"For what?"

"For helping me realize how cool she is." He shook his head. "I was really wrong about her."

I looked away. "Sure. No problem."

Just then his mother came out, jingling her keys in her hand. "You kids ready to go?"

Of course, I love animals, so I was excited about getting to walk dogs and snuggle with cats at the shelter, but I was also excited about seeing my dad at work. Most of the time he was at his new veterinary practice, but he hadn't given up his commitment to spend two Sundays a month at the shelter as a volunteer vet. I was so proud of him for what he did for the shelter, and I wanted him to be proud of me, too. That we could both be volunteers there made it feel extra special. Also, since I hardly saw him during the week, I was really looking forward to spending time with him.

Too bad *that* didn't happen. When we'd arrived, I'd asked about him and they'd told me he was doing surgeries all day, so I probably wouldn't see him at all. Sure enough, four hours, five dog walks, and countless kitty snuggles later I had seen my dad for a total of zero minutes.

The good news was that I quickly got so busy with taking care of the animals that I soon forgot about quality father-daughter time. I barely even saw Tyler, we were so busy.

Before I knew it, I'd returned the last dog to her kennel. One glance at the clock told me it was after two—time to turn in my volunteer badge. When I got to the desk, Tyler was already there, signing out. He handed me the pen.

"Thanks," I said, taking it from him and signing my name on the line before I passed the volunteer coordinator my badge.

"How was your day?" Tyler asked.

I blew out a loud breath. "Really great. But I must have walked like twenty miles! I'm zonked. How about you?"

He grinned at me. "I know, right? Same. I can't wait to plant myself on the couch and play Slashers. You coming over?"

I wanted to play with him and have it be like we used to be before the summer. But I also *didn't* want to, because I was nervous around him now—because of the whole Olivia thing and also because I was scared that if I played with him, he'd figure out it hadn't been Olivia at the controller. Would we ever get to hang out again the way we used to?

I opened my mouth to tell him that my thumb still hurt and that I had too much homework to do, but I didn't have a chance to speak.

"There you are," my father said in his booming voice. "Hi, Kat, Tyler."

I turned around and smiled at my dad, who was coming toward us. He looked tired.

"Hi, Dad. We didn't get to see you at all today!"

"Sorry, Kat," he said. "It was crazy back there. You know they don't have a regular vet here through the week, so I had to make up for it today. Twenty-seven cats came in this week, and at least a dozen dogs . . ." He sighed.

"Wow, I didn't realize so many!"

"It's a busy place. Come on, let's get out of here." He put his arm around me, and the three of us walked toward the door. "You must have been busy." He glanced over his shoulder at Tyler. "Both of you—I know how they work their volunteers around here. So what do you think?"

"It was so cool," Tyler said. "I like helping out. Even the gross stuff—like cleaning the litter boxes—doesn't bother me."

"Me too," I said. "I love being around the animals. But it was so much work; we're exhausted!"

Dad squeezed me into his side. "It's not always good times, but I'm glad you liked it. I'm sure both of you were a big help today."

I looked up at my dad, and he smiled back. "I think you two have earned something special. Your choice: ice cream or cupcakes?"

I looked at Tyler and he looked at me before we said at the same time, "Ice cream!"

"Great," Dad said as we made our way outside and toward his car. "We'll go to Scoops, and then after I take you two home, I'll still have time to get a few hours of work done at the clinic before dinner."

I stopped at the car door. "What do you mean? You're not coming home?"

"Sorry, honey," Dad said, opening his door and getting into the car. He waited until we were inside and buckled up before he went on. "Just because I volunteer here doesn't mean the work at my clinic stops. I have a lot to catch up on."

"You should get a break, though," I said. "It's Sunday; the clinic isn't even open!"

He sighed. "It's different when it's your own business. I do so much more than just taking care of animals. Paperwork. Staff scheduling. Billing."

"But you're never around. And you're probably going to be late for dinner. Again."

"Kat . . ." He looked at Tyler in the mirror, and I knew he didn't want me to say things in front of him, but I couldn't help it. Dad worked too much; I wasn't the only one who thought so.

"But you're late all the time." I didn't mean for my voice to come out sounding so whiny, but it did.

"Kat. Let's talk about this later, okay?" His voice wasn't mad, exactly, but I could tell he wasn't happy.

I looked out the window and fought the tears that wanted to come. The silence in the car felt weird, but there wasn't anything else I could say that wouldn't make Dad angry.

"Kat?" Tyler said from the back seat. "Why don't you bring your homework over when we get home? We can work on math together."

"Okay," I said, hating that my voice was kind of squeaky but liking that he still wanted me to come over. And that maybe he understood that what I really needed right then, if I couldn't have my dad, was a best friend. "Thanks."

Later, after we had ice cream and Dad dropped us off, I told Tyler I was exhausted and needed a nap, so I never did go over with my homework. He seemed disappointed and I wanted to tell him that it meant a lot that he'd invited me, but didn't know how to without explaining that it was too weird.

He texted me later that night when I was actually struggling through the homework on my own, but I lied and told him Laura had helped me with it and I was all done. I felt bad about lying to him, and I'm not even sure he believed me, but how could I explain why I couldn't be alone with him?

Chapter 10

ON TUESDAY MORNING IN FIRST PERIOD, WE WERE supposed to be writing in our daily journals (I was actually staring at the wall, thinking about *Hector: Ninja Cat*) when a folded-up paper landed on my notebook. It startled me, but when I saw it was a note, I covered up my movement with a pretend shiver. A glance at the teacher—Ms. Ghosh—told me she hadn't noticed and was busy looking at her iPad.

I looked over in the direction it had come from and wasn't surprised to see Zoe—one of my not-best-friend friends—smiling at me and looking excited. Clearly, she was behind whatever was on that paper.

I glanced over on the other side of me at Livvy. She waggled her eyebrows and then looked down at the paper in front of me—her way of telling me silently to look at it. She and Zoe walked to school together sometimes, so I had a feeling that, whatever it was, both of them were in on it.

I coughed to cover up the crinkling of the paper as I unfolded the note.

!!!! PRIVATE !!!!

IF YOUR NAME IS NOT ZOE, OLIVIA, KAT, OR JASMINE, DO NOT READ.

If your name IS Zoe, Olivia, Kat, or Jasmine, you must be honest or you will be cursed for all of eternity!

Who is your crush? _____

Why? _____

Does he like you? _____

Are you going to the dance with him? _____

How many times will you dance with him? (slow songs) _____

How many times will you dance with him? (fast songs) _____

What are you wearing to the dance? _____

Once you are done, pass your quiz to the next person.

IF YOU ARE NOT ZOE, OLIVIA, KAT, OR JASMINE AND YOU HAVE READ THIS FAR, YOU WILL BE CURSED FOR ALL OF ETERNITY!!!

Ugh. So I was supposed to answer this and then pass it to Livvy so she could fill it out and then pass it on to Jasmine. While I realized Zoe had put a lot of work into this, there was no way I was filling this out. Not in a million years. I'd rather be cursed for all of eternity.

So instead of doing it, I smiled at Zoe, folded up the paper, and, after checking to make sure Ms. Ghosh wasn't looking, tossed it to Olivia.

Olivia grabbed it and was going to toss it back to me, mouthing, *YOU first!* but I quickly shook my head.

No, I mouthed back to her.

You have to!

Uh, no I don't, I thought, looking toward the front of the room and especially avoiding looking at Tyler, who sat two seats behind me in the next row over. Olivia continued to try to get my attention: coughing, fake sneezing, tapping her foot. When none of that worked, she asked if she could go to the bathroom, which I knew was a sign that I should meet her there so we could talk.

My responses to her attempts to get my attention were, in order: (1) ignore, (2) say "gesundheit," (3) ignore, and (4) stay in my seat.

Instead I returned to my journal. I was going to write about my first day working at the shelter, but I was so frazzled about the quiz/note that I couldn't focus very well. Why had Zoe included me anyway? She knew I didn't care about this stuff.

A few minutes later Olivia returned to the room, and I could feel her glaring at me as she walked down the row toward our desks. She sat heavily in her chair, letting out a big sigh.

"Olivia, is there a problem?" Ms. Ghosh said, sounding annoyed.

"No, Ms. Ghosh," Livvy said.

"Well, then, back to your journal entry," the teacher said. "Ten more minutes, everyone."

But instead of returning to her writing, Olivia slipped the folded note out of her book and opened it. She turned her head toward me, and I resisted looking at her, watching out of the corner of my eye as she started filling it out. Several looooong minutes later—while I waited for her to finish—the note landed in front of me again.

I turned toward Olivia. *No!* I mouthed.

Why? she mouthed back.

Why? Ugh. I couldn't even tell her why I wouldn't—couldn't—fill it out. I tried to make my face not be so hot, but I might as well have willed myself to sprout wings and fly out of the classroom.

She nodded toward the paper. Well, I guessed I could at least see what she'd written. But did I really want to? Curiosity got the best of me, and I slowly unfolded the note as quietly as possible.

!!!! PRIVATE !!!!

IF YOUR NAME IS NOT ZOE, OLIVIA, KAT, OR JASMINE, DO NOT READ.

If your name IS Zoe, Olivia, Kat, or Jasmine, you must be honest or you will be cursed for all of eternity!

Who is your crush? TYLER LOT

Why?   SO cute. Popular. Great hair.

Does he like you? Don't know?????

Are you going to the dance with him? Y (Right, Kat?)

How many times will you dance with him? (slow songs) All of them

How many times will you dance with him? (fast songs) All of them

What are you wearing to the dance? <u>A new
dress!</u>

Once you are done, pass your quiz to the
next person.

IF YOU ARE NOT ZOE, OLIVIA, KAT, OR JASMINE
AND YOU HAVE READ THIS FAR, YOU WILL BE
CURSED FOR ALL OF ETERNITY!!!

I sighed. Now what?

"You have to do it," Zoe whispered.

I glanced over at her and shook my head.

"You have to!"

I looked down at the paper, knowing there was no
way out of it. I had a choice to make: I could make up
fibs and be cursed for all of eternity, or I could tell the
truth and be humiliated for all of eternity.

Obviously, I picked cursed.

!!!! PRIVATE !!!!

IF YOUR NAME IS NOT ZOE, OLIVIA, KAT, OR
JASMINE, DO NOT READ.

If your name IS Zoe, Olivia, Kat, or Jasmine, you must be honest or you will be cursed for all of eternity!

Who is your crush? TYLER LOT Hector N. Cat

Why? SO cute. Popular. Cute.   Ninja Skills

Does he like you? Don't know?????   Y. Especially at feeding time

Are you going to the dance with him? Y (Right. Kat?) He doesn't dance—2 left feet. Ha ha ha.

How many times will you dance with him? (slow songs) All of them   Does not apply

How many times will you dance with him? (fast songs) All of them   Does not apply

What are you wearing to the dance? A new dress!   Does not apply

Once you are done, pass your quiz to the next person.

IF YOU ARE NOT ZOE, OLIVIA, KAT, OR JASMINE
AND YOU HAVE READ THIS FAR, YOU WILL BE
CURSED FOR ALL OF ETERNITY!!!

I finished and folded up the paper, wondering how I was supposed to get it to Jasmine, who was way at the front of the room. There was no way I trusted any other kids to pass it along without reading it. I was about to put up my hand to ask to use the bathroom so I could drop it on her desk when Olivia leaned over and snatched it right off my desk.

I almost yelled out, "Hey!" but managed to stop myself. Luckily, Ms. Ghosh didn't seem to notice that anything was amiss. I couldn't do anything but watch as Olivia unfolded the note and read it before she looked at me.

"Really?"

I shrugged and grinned at her.

She rolled her eyes. *No one?* she mouthed, asking for my real answer to the questions.

I shook my head. It was a lie, but I couldn't tell her the truth.

Over on the other side of the room TJ Stevens twirled his pen, drawing my attention. Apparently Olivia saw that as some sort of confession or something, because she turned and followed my eyes, then looked back at me. *TJ?*

I shook my head vigorously. *No,* I mouthed. *Not TJ.*

She tilted her head and lifted her eyebrows as if to say, *Really?*

Really, I mouthed. *No crush on ANYONE.*

She stared at me for a long, tense minute, and I didn't think she was going to let it go. Finally, when I was ready to scream, she shrugged and folded the paper back up before she shoved it in her notebook— she'd have to wait until later to pass it to Jasmine.

I had never felt so relieved in all my life!

It had been a busy week for me, what with homework, dodging my sister, proving I didn't have a crush on ANYONE, shelving books in the library, and trying to find time to work on my manga, so by the time Thursday came, I couldn't believe the week was almost over. Although I couldn't forget that the Fall Ball was in just over a week; I had Olivia's many reminders of that fact.

Mostly because Tyler hadn't asked her yet, and she was beginning to panic.

"Kat," she said at lunch in the cafeteria before he arrived, "is he *ever* going to ask me?"

I glanced up from my gross tuna sandwich, which might as well have been a *mayo* sandwich (thanks to my dear older sister), and at Olivia, who looked like she was about to have a major meltdown.

"Why don't *you* ask *him*?" I suggested. "That was your original plan, wasn't it?"

She looked down at the non-sister-made sandwich in her hands. "Yeah, I guess. I just . . . I can't tell if he likes me."

I laughed, making her look up at me.

"What? What's so funny, Kat?"

"Have you looked in a mirror? I mean, you're so beautiful and graceful and everything. . . ."

She frowned and put down her sandwich. "What does that mean?"

Uh-oh. She actually looked upset. "I'm not trying to be mean, Livvy. Just that you're . . ."

"What?"

"I don't know. I guess I never thought *you* would ever have to worry about if a boy likes you. You're kind of perfect."

"What? No I'm not," she said, her voice so quiet I almost didn't hear her over all the noise in the cafeteria. "I'm not smart or artistic like you, and I don't like books or all that stuff Tyler likes. You even said so yourself."

She seemed really upset, and I hated that; I'd never meant to hurt her feelings. "But you've been reading and trying some of it. And please, I would give all of my drawing ability to be tall and graceful"—*like a gazelle,* I finished in my head.

She shrugged. "I guess . . . I . . ."

"Hey, Livvy!" Tyler said, dropping into the seat next to her, cutting off our conversation. I was relieved and sad at the same time. I didn't want her to feel upset about things.

But as I glanced over at her, I noticed her face lit up as soon as he spoke to her.

"Hi!" she said. "Oh, I forgot to tell you, Kat. I filled

out the online application for the animal shelter, and they said I could start this Sunday!"

It was the first I'd heard of her actually going through with applying. "Are you sure you want to do that?"

She gave me a quick look that said, *Shhh!* and then turned to Tyler. "I'm so excited to get started there. You know, I actually have a lot of experience with animals."

You do? I thought, but kept my mouth shut.

"Oh yeah?" Tyler said as he pulled his lunch bag from his backpack.

"Yeah," Olivia said. "My uncle has a farm with all sorts of animals: pigs, sheep, goats, and chickens. I worked there over the summer."

I couldn't believe the story she was making up. I mean, it was true about her uncle (on her mom's side of the family) having a farm, and yes, she had spent some time there over the summer, but it had been like four days and she'd never left the ranch house the whole time! She'd texted me several times a day to tell me about all the shows she was watching on Netflix!

"That's so cool," Tyler said, obviously impressed. "Dogs and cats are probably way easier to take care of than farm animals."

Olivia smiled and did a little wave. "They'll be no problem. I'm something of an expert."

An expert fibber, *maybe.*

"Tho hey," Tyler slurred after he took a huge bite of sandwich. A sandwich that even had lettuce on it, lucky guy. "Do you want to come over and play Slashers tonight?"

Olivia's eyes went wide in alarm as she looked at me, but she was worrying for nothing.

"Livvy can't; she has dance-team practice," I said.

"Oh yeah!" she said, obviously relieved. "I forgot about that. Why don't you come watch?"

I almost laughed, because I knew for sure that Tyler would never be interested in watching a dance team. Not in a million years.

"Sure! That would be great," he said, and then looked at me. "You'll come too, right?"

I just stared at him for what felt like several very long seconds. He was smiling at me like dance was his new favorite thing and *of course* he'd want to go watch a bunch of gazelles practice.

"Oh, sure," I said. "That sounds awesome."

"Yay!" Olivia clapped her hands, a big grin on her face. She looked like she was about to bust out a cheer, but then seemed to realize what she was doing. She stopped clapping suddenly, quickly grabbed her sandwich, and took a bite.

Tyler was watching her, but the way he was smiling at her, I could tell he just thought it was another one of her adorable quirks. Not what it really was: an attempt to dampen her over-the-top enthusiasm because I had told her he didn't like that kind of thing.

As I watched her, I felt bad for ever having told her to not be herself around Tyler. One of the things I loved about her was how bubbly and excited she got about things. But she was the one who wanted my help in getting Tyler to really notice her—in a good way—so getting her to bring herself down a notch (or ten) was important.

Still, it felt like she was taking away the best parts of who she was to make him notice her, and while it was what she *said* she wanted, I couldn't help but wonder if she even really understood what that meant.

Later that night (after Livvy's dance-team practice and another cold, late dinner, thanks to Dad) I was working on my manga in the kitchen, trying to get Ninja Hector just right, when I got a text from Tyler.

Tyler: *want to come over?*

I glanced at the clock on the microwave before I texted back. I only had an hour before bedtime. He knew that, so it was kind of weird that he'd invite me over now.

Kat: *it's too late to play.*

Tyler: *ok.*

I could see he was typing by the three dots on the screen, but for the longest time no words came up. I waited.

And waited.

Then waited some more. Until I couldn't stand it anymore.

Kat: *??*

Tyler: *Can I ask U a ?*

Kat: *Yep.*

My heart started to pound in my chest. I couldn't think of what he was going to ask, but I knew it had to be serious if he was *asking* if he could ask. That wasn't like him. But my thumping, nervous heart knew: He was probably going to bust me and Olivia for all the ways she'd pretended to be someone she wasn't and how I'd been her accomplice.

Tyler: . . .

Tyler: . . .

My head was about to explode from waiting, when his text finally came through.

Tyler: *Are you avoiding me?*

Okay, that was not *at all* what I had expected. But it made my heart pound as much as if he'd figured out what Olivia and I were doing. Because I *was* avoiding him. Sort of. Mostly because I couldn't play Zombie Slashers with him without letting on that I'd pretended to be Olivia. Also there was that whole thing about how cute he'd gotten over the summer and how it made me feel squiggly inside to be around him, especially if it was just us. Just to be clear, squiggly isn't a really good feeling. Especially when he and Olivia were like ten seconds away from being a couple. Which was what I wanted, of course—because if they were a couple, he and I would go back to being just friends, and my stupid crush feelings would go away.

As all of this went through my head, my phone vibrated in my hand, startling me out of my thoughts.

Tyler: *Kat? You there?*

Kat: *ya, sorry. Just talking to mom. No. not avoiding you.*

Tyler: *you sure? You havnt been over to play video games and the scavenger hunt . . .*

Kat: *Just busy, Ty. NBD.*

Tyler: *ok. So we are good?*

Kat: *of course, nerd*

Tyler: *lol, dork :P*

I smiled at that. Even though I felt bad about all the pretending. It felt weird, but in the end he and Olivia would be together, so it would all be okay.

Right?

Kat: *I should go. Working on my manga*

Tyler: *when do I get to see it?*

I thought about it. I really wanted to show it to

him, but not yet. I had always been good at art, and he'd seen my very first Hector drawing, but this was my first try at doing a whole graphic novel, and it was going pretty slow.

Kat: *soon.*

Tyler: *can't wait.*

That made me feel good; I knew he wasn't just faking wanting to see it. We'd talked about the storyline already—he'd helped me figure that part out—so I felt like I sort of owed it to him to show him the artwork. But I really wanted him to be impressed, which meant I needed to make sure it was as good as I could get it.

Kat: *better go. See you tomorrow.*

Tyler: *C U bye*

Chapter 11

"ARE YOU SURE YOU WANT TO DO THIS?" I ASKED Olivia.

It was Sunday, her mom had just dropped her off at my place, and we were in the kitchen putting together snacks to take with us to the animal shelter. Tyler was due to arrive in ten minutes, and then my mom would be driving us; Dad had already left to spend the day at his clinic, since this wasn't one of his volunteer Sundays. Before that happened, though, I thought I should give her one last chance to back out.

She paused in slicing an apple and looked up at me. "Am I sure I want to do what?"

"Volunteer at the shelter."

She rolled her eyes. "Uh, yeah. I signed up for it."

I did an eye-roll of my own. "I know, but you don't exactly love animals."

"I can pretend," she said very matter-of-factly.

"Okay, but you don't just *not love* animals," I said, looking her in the eye so she would really understand. "You are *afraid* of animals. How are you going to manage that?"

What I *really* meant was, *How are you going to not squeal and freak out if a big dog comes near you?* It wasn't that I blamed her for her fear of dogs—Great Danes are huge and I understood how she could be scarred for life after being knocked down by Uncle Fred's—but it seemed kind of stupid for her to pretend she wasn't afraid and go out of her way to be around animals.

Olivia returned to slicing the apple and shrugged. "I'll figure it out. Tyler obviously likes animals, so I need to too. Plus"—she looked up at me again—"the dance is *this* Friday, and he hasn't asked me yet. I need to be around him every second so he has the opportunity. I need to make this happen."

She still didn't seem sure enough to invite him to the dance herself, so I knew where she was coming from, but still, the animal-shelter thing seemed like a bad idea.

"Maybe stay near the cats," I said. "You'll probably do better with smaller animals."

"But they have claws," she said. "Do they have any bunny rabbits? Maybe I could do something with rabbits. Although they poop a lot, don't they?"

I looked at my cousin and her scrunched-up face as she thought about rabbit poop.

Yeah, this is such a bad idea, I thought. *Like, epically bad.*

Tyler showed up a little while later, let himself into the house like he always did, and followed the voices to find us in the kitchen.

"Oh, hi, Tyler!" Olivia said, gliding over to him, carrying the package of oatmeal-raisin cookies I'd made for him. "I remembered oatmeal-raisin is your favorite."

He smiled at her and even blushed a little as he thanked her. He took the cookies and stuffed them into his pocket. "So, you excited for today?" he asked.

I looked at Olivia, wondering how she was going to answer, but before she got the chance, Mom rushed into the room, keys in hand and purse over her shoulder. "Okay, let's go," she said, not even slowing down on her way to the garage door.

Olivia turned and followed as though she'd been distracted away from Tyler's question. But I had a suspicion she'd used the interruption as an excuse to not have to answer.

We piled into the car—me in front and Tyler and Olivia in the back—and buckled in for the short drive to the animal shelter. Mom and Olivia talked about the latest episode of *Dancing with the Stars*, discussing who should win this season. I had no idea who the people were that they were talking about, so I turned in my seat and rolled my eyes at Tyler. He grinned back at me and then pushed his fingers through his hair. But that little piece fell back down onto his forehead, and I had to turn back around to look out the front or he was going to see me blushing.

Finally, we arrived at the shelter. The three of us

got out of the car after Mom promised she'd be back at two. We led Olivia toward the volunteer desk to sign in and get our badges.

I barely even noticed the echoes of all the dogs barking—we'd gotten used to it quickly last week—but it was all new for Olivia, who had never set foot in a shelter before that moment.

"Gah! It's so loud in here!" she yelled, pressing her hands over her ears.

I exchanged glances with Tyler. Yeah it was loud, but that was all part of it. What did she think, that a shelter full of dogs was going to be like a library?

"You'll get used to it," he said to her. "Come on, we'd better sign in."

Olivia gave me a sideways look that I knew meant *Help me!* but what could I do? I'd warned her and had even given her a last chance to bail, but here she was anyway. Maybe I could try to make the best of it for her somehow.

I stepped ahead of her at the sign-up desk. "Hi," I said to Justine, the volunteer coordinator I remembered from the week before. "This is Olivia—today's her first day. Maybe she should start off in the cat room?"

Justine smiled at Olivia as she got badges out of a drawer and slid them across the desk at us. "Welcome, Olivia. A cat lover, are you?"

Olivia quickly glanced at Tyler before she smiled at Justine. "Oh yes. Very much. The only thing I like better than cats are bunny rabbits. Do you have any rabbits?"

Justine blinked at her a few times before she said, "Actually, we do. But the early-morning crew has already taken care of them."

"What do you need done today?" Tyler asked.

Justine smiled at him. "What *don't* we need done?" she said with a wink before she picked up a clipboard in front of her. "All right. I need dogs walked, floors mopped, and kennels cleaned."

"I'll mop floors!" Olivia said quickly.

Justine laughed, her eyebrows high up on her head. "I've never had anyone so enthusiastic about mopping, but who am I to judge?"

I grabbed my badge and clipped it to my shirt, then handed Olivia one for her to do the same. "I'll walk," I said.

Tyler signed in last and then said, "I guess that leaves me to the kennels."

"We can swap out halfway," I said, because it was only fair. Walking the dogs was the best part of being a volunteer.

He smiled at me. "Thanks."

"You remember where you're going, Kat?" Justine asked.

I pointed toward the hallway that led to the kennels. "Yep, thanks."

"All righty," she said. "Don't forget to mark down in the log who you walk. I'll show Olivia and Tyler where the cleaning supplies are."

I was reluctant to leave them, knowing Olivia was totally out of her comfort zone, but I had no choice. Anyway, like Dad always said, she'd made her bed; now it was time for her to lie in it.

About a half hour later I was walking Ranger—a Labradoodle—when my phone rang in my pocket. I ignored it, but the second it went to voice mail it started to ring again, so I figured whoever was calling really wanted to get a hold of me.

Olivia, I thought instantly. I stopped in my tracks and gave Ranger a bit of slack on the leash so he could sniff around while I answered the call.

Sure enough, her name came up on my screen. I answered it right away.

"Hey" was barely out of my mouth when I heard an ear-piercing screech that made me hold the phone away from my face. (I could still hear her.)

"I need your help!"

I waited half a second to make sure she was done yelling before I brought the phone to my ear. "What's going on?" I asked, and then immediately held the phone away.

"There's a *PIG* here!" she hollered.

"What?"

"A pig!"

"A pig?"

"Yes! A pig! You know, oink, oink, pork chops and bacon."

I pictured a huge pink animal like we'd seen at the fair last year, but that didn't seem right. I couldn't imagine there being a giant pig at the shelter. And then I remembered that my Dad had had this client back at the old vet office where he used to work. . . .

"Wait, Livvy, do you mean a pot-bellied pig? Like someone's pet?"

"Yes! That's what I said! A pig! Someone dropped it off at the lost and found when I was cleaning the floor. It was running around squealing and going nuts and then it—ugh!—*POOPED* on the floor I'd just washed! Then it ran *through* the poop . . ." I heard her start to gag, and though I felt really bad, I couldn't help but laugh a little.

"Kat, I swear . . . it's *NOT FUNNY*! There are smeared poopy pig prints all over, and it stinks *so* bad!"

That just made it funnier, but she was freaking out, so I tried to hold it in for her sake. "No, it's not funny. I'm sorry, Livvy. But I'm at least twenty minutes away; what do you want me to do?"

"Help me figure out how to handle this! Justine is at lunch, the other volunteers are busy, and Tyler thinks I know about pigs because I told him about the farm, but I don't know anything . . . and . . . I . . ." Her voice trailed off, and I could tell she was starting to cry.

"Livvy, calm down. Where is the pig now?"

"I don't know. Out in the hall, I guess."

"Where are you?"

"In the bathroom."

I sighed. "Okay. You're going to have to go out there and act calm. If *you're* freaking out, the pig is going to freak out too. They're really sensitive." My pig knowledge wasn't exactly extensive, but I knew enough about animals from my dad to make an educated guess.

"I don't think I can do it, Kat," she whined.

"Livvy, yes you can. You just need to focus. Now breathe."

I heard her take a few deep breaths.

"Good," I said. "Now listen to me. You need to go out there and secure the pig. If the floor was wet, it might have scared him a little. He's probably not used to sliding around on slippery surfaces, so maybe that's why he started going nuts. Does he have a collar on or something you can grab on to?"

"I . . . I think he was wearing a harness," she said.

"Okay, good. So what you need to do is be *very* calm and see if you can grab his harness and lead him into one of the dog kennels. Talk in a soothing voice to calm him down. He will quiet down more quickly if he's in a smaller space and can't run around too much."

"You sure?"

No, but I wasn't about to tell her that. I figured that at least if the pig was locked in a kennel, he couldn't hurt her or himself. "Yes," I said. "But the key is to be *really calm*. Can you do that?"

"I . . . I'll try," she said.

Suddenly I heard squealing through the phone, and then someone shouted, "Olivia! Where are you?"

"Oh no, that's Tyler!" she hissed.

"You'd better go," I said as I tugged on the leash to get Ranger's attention so we could start walking back to the shelter. "I'm on my way back. Just be calm, Livvy. You've got this."

"Okay, but please hurry!"

I started to jog, the excited Ranger matching my pace. "I'm coming as fast as I can!"

*

"You should have seen her!" Tyler said, his eyes wide with awe.

I'd just returned to the shelter and put Ranger away when Olivia and Tyler greeted me to tell me what had happened with the arrival of the pot-bellied pig, as if it was the first I was hearing about the ordeal. "At first I thought she was freaking out and hiding, but then she came out of the bathroom and handled that pig like a boss!"

I looked at my best cousin, and yeah, she was smiling like crazy, obviously basking in Tyler's praise and attention.

"Well, I wanted to make sure my hands were clean before I handled the pig," she said, like she hadn't, in fact, been hiding in the bathroom calling me in a total panic and instead had had the whole situation under control from the beginning. "You don't want to spread disease. And in a shelter environment, that's *especially* important."

Okay, so obviously she'd read the little notice by the bathroom sink about the importance of hand washing. But I had to say, she sure did sound like she knew what she was talking about. She'd never mentioned wanting to be an actress before, but I had a feeling it was a career she could totally nail.

"You were *so* calm," Tyler said to her. "I had no idea what to do. I'm so glad you have all that farm experience. That really came in handy!"

"Of course," she said, waving him off like it was no big deal.

Right. "Where is the pig now?" I asked, looking around.

"Livvy put him in one of the kennels. We notified one of the techs, and she's going to check him out and give him a bath."

"I was going to—give him a bath, I mean," Olivia said. "But the floor was such a mess and I didn't want it to get worse."

Her smile faltered a bit then; she covered it up quickly, but I could tell that she was struggling to keep it together. The whole pig and pig's *mess* was way more than she had signed up for, but if she had to choose between the two, a mop and a bucket would win out over a squealing swine anytime.

"That makes sense," I said encouragingly. "Best to let them deal with the pig anyway. Where did he come from?"

"Someone dropped him off in the lost-and-found area," Tyler said. "Just dumped him there and left—no one even knew he was there until he started running around squealing. Poor guy."

"Any word on his owner?" I asked.

"No," Tyler said. "Do they microchip pigs?"

I shrugged. "No idea, but I'm sure they'll scan him for one if they do." I really wanted to check him out, because I'd never actually seen a pot-bellied pig before, but while I wasn't as bothered by the kind of dirty things that came with being an animal lover as Olivia was, I didn't exactly want to play with a poopy pig.

"Hey, you did great today," Tyler said suddenly. He was looking at Olivia, and—wait a minute—was he making googly eyes at her? Yes, he was. He was totally staring at her *that way*. It bothered me a little, which was stupid, because getting him to like her was exactly what we were doing all this for: Project Ty-Livia.

I looked at her and she was looking at . . . her shirt. She pulled at the bottom and held it out from her body. "Ugh, I think I have . . . *ew*!" She slapped her hand over her mouth and ran for the bathroom.

"Poor Olivia," I muttered.

"Huh?" Tyler said, reminding me he was right there.

"Uh . . . just that her first shift here was so . . . eventful!"

"She did great, though. I mean, I really don't know what I would have done with that pig if it wasn't for her," he said. "Crisis averted."

"Yeah. Well, I guess I should go walk the next dog. Unless you want to switch?"

He glanced toward the bathroom that Olivia had disappeared into, and then back at me. "I'm okay. I'll just keep doing what I'm doing."

"All right, I'll get back to it then," I said, turning back toward the kennels.

"Hey, Kat?"

I turned back again. "Yeah?"

He stepped close. Really close. "Do you think . . ." He looked over his shoulder and then back at me. "Do you think Olivia . . . would she . . . do you think she'd want to go to the dance with me?"

"I thought you didn't want to go!" The words came out before I could stop them, and I actually clamped my hand over my mouth. "I mean," I added, trying not to sound like I was bonkers, "you didn't seem interested before."

He shrugged. "Well, uh, I guess that was before I got to know Olivia better." He paused. "So, do you think she would go with me?"

My breath caught in my lungs a little, and I stood there trying to figure out what I was feeling, because I should have been happy for Olivia, but . . . Then I realized he was standing there, staring at me and waiting for my answer. "Uh . . . yeah, I'm pretty sure she would."

He nodded. "I think I like her."

"Of course you do," I said, despite the lump in my throat. "She's so beautiful and graceful and fun and all that. Why *wouldn't* you like her?"

He frowned. "That's not why I like her, Kat. I like her because she's into all the same stuff I like. I like that she remembered oatmeal-raisin cookies are my favorite and that she has no problem kicking my butt at Zombie Slashers. And she's got real opinions about the Blackwood Knights books. She's pretty, sure," he said, his eyes dropping from mine as his face suddenly got really red, "but no prettier than you."

"What?" came out of my mouth before I even realized. But seriously, what had he just said? My face was burning hot, and I was sure I looked like a big red idiot.

"I should go," he said suddenly. "I have a lot of kennels to clean before we leave today."

And then he was gone.

"What just happened?" I asked the empty hallway. "Did he just say I was as pretty as Olivia?" I shook my head, convinced I was hearing things. Tyler had never looked at me that way. I would have noticed. Wouldn't I have?

But as I made my way toward where I would pick up my next dog to walk, what he'd said started to roll around in my head. All the reasons why he liked Olivia were exactly the things that made him and me friends.

I stopped and looked back down the hallway

toward where he'd gone. Could Tyler and I have . . . ?

At that moment Olivia came out of the bathroom, a big wet spot on her shirt where she'd cleaned it. "Gross," she said, wrinkling her nose. "Where's Tyler?"

I pointed. "Off cleaning kennels." I almost told her he was going to ask her to the dance, but maybe it was best if she heard it from him anyway.

"Thanks for everything, Kat," she said.

I nodded and watched her follow down the hallway where he'd gone.

Chapter 12

MOM DROPPED OLIVIA OFF ON THE WAY HOME from the shelter, leaving just me and Tyler in the car with her.

I knew Tyler hadn't asked Olivia to the dance yet, because, knowing her, she would have been bursting with the news and would have dragged me into the bathroom before we left the building to tell me immediately.

So he hadn't yet asked her, but he was planning to.

I couldn't tell if he felt weird about the conversation we'd had back at the shelter, but I sure did. Thankfully, sitting in the front seat meant I didn't have to look at him at all. Just to make sure, I asked my mom a million questions about dinner: what were we having (chicken, potatoes, and salad) and then the ingredient listing of the salad and if she knew what was in the dressing. Then I asked her to describe how she made scalloped potatoes as though I was taking notes for a cookbook.

She took her eyes off the road long enough to smirk at me. "Why the sudden interest in all the cooking? You starting a restaurant?"

"No," I said. "I'm just curious, that's all."

"Your potatoes sound *really* delicious," Tyler said from the back seat.

Mom smiled in the mirror at him. "They're my specialty. I can't believe you've never had them. Want to come for dinner?"

I was about to say that he had homework to do or something (and that of course he'd had the potatoes before, because he had, many, *many* times), but he spoke before I got the chance.

"That would be great, thanks. My parents are out at a fund-raiser anyway."

"Oh? For what?" Mom asked him. She was sort of friends with Tyler's mom, and his parents used to go out with my parents sometimes, but since Dad had started his practice, they almost never went out anymore.

"The historical society," Tyler answered. "It's a fancy dinner and dance. They're getting all dressed up. Dad even had to rent a tuxedo."

Mom nodded and then looked at the road, but I could see the sadness in her eyes and the way she gripped the steering wheel really tightly. *She* wanted to get dressed up too.

"Maybe after dinner we can watch a movie," I said, trying to make her feel better.

"That sounds nice, Kat," she said. "We haven't all sat down to watch a movie in a while. You'll join us too, Tyler?"

"I have some homework to finish, but if I can get that done before dinner, then yeah. Thanks."

Great. So not only was he coming over for dinner, but I was going to have to sit with him through an entire movie, knowing he was going to ask Olivia to the dance.

And there wasn't one thing I could do about it.

*

Five minutes after Tyler got out of Mom's car and promised he'd return in time for dinner, I got a text from Olivia.

Olivia: *HE JUST ASKED ME!*

Kat: *You don't have to yell!*

Olivia: *SORRY!*

I rolled my eyes.

Kat: *What did you say?*

Olivia: *HILARIUS. OF COURSE I SAID YES.*

It was hard not to smile at her goofy texts. She was obviously crazy excited about it, and I was happy for her.

Mostly. Sort of.

Olivia: *I mean, I will. As soon as you tell me what to say.*

Kat: *What are you talking about? Just say yes.*

Olivia: *shouldn't I say it in some special way or something?*

"You're nuts," I said out loud, shaking my head.

Kat: *stop thinking so much. Just say yes.*

Olivia: *ok. youre going to come to the dance?*

I laughed out loud at that one.

Kat: no.

Olivia: *pleeeeeeeze*

Kat: *no. I'm busy.*

Olivia: *doing what?*

Not going to the dance, I thought. I dialed her instead of texting back.

"Livvy, I'm not going to the dance. That was never part of the deal. And anyway, I'd just be in the way."

"No you won't!" Her voice was panicked. "You can dance with TJ."

I sighed. "I told you, I don't like him."

"But . . . I . . . what do I—"

"Livvy, it's no different than being with Tyler at school. You'll do fine."

"Not if you're not there."

"Just study your notes."

I could almost hear her pouting over the phone. I was relieved when she sighed and said, "Fine. All right."

"And remember, this is a dance—it's your element."

"I guess . . . but don't you think if you—"

Not this again! "I've gotta go," I said, cutting her

off. "I promised Mom I'd help her make dinner."

Especially since I'd gone on and on about the scalloped potatoes recipe and now knew it by heart.

"Okay, I'll see you tomorrow, Kat. Seriously, I can't thank you enough for this! I'm going to pay you back somehow. I'm *so* excited!"

I was barely off the phone with her when I got another text. I thought it was going to be her again, but when I looked at the screen, my stomach fluttered.

Tyler: *she said yes.*

Sigh.

Kat: *of course she did. I told you she would.*

Tyler: ☺ *see you at dinner.*

Right. Dinner. Awesome.

Chapter 13

I THOUGHT THE DAYS LEADING UP TO THE DANCE
would be filled with awkwardness as Tyler and
Olivia tried to not be weird about going to the dance
together. Instead it seemed like both of them had
decided to pretty much ignore each other. I thought
that was weird, but Olivia was mostly concerned with
her dress and how she would look and Tyler was more
concerned with . . . well, I didn't know what he was
concerned with, because I barely saw him. At lunch he
sat with some guys from homeroom.

I felt bad about that, but it was kind of a relief,
because while *Olivia and Tyler* didn't seem to be feeling

awkward, I sure was. I couldn't wait for it all to be over. I'd had to listen to Olivia go on and on about her dress and shoes (I'd suggested that maybe wearing heels when she was *already* taller than Tyler wasn't the best idea, but *she* said the shoes went with the dress and that was the most important thing, so whatever) and her appointments for her hair and nails. She'd asked if I wanted to come with her to the salon just for fun, but I didn't see much point in getting myself made up when I'd just be sitting at home in front of the TV anyway. She gave me a long look, and I could tell she wanted to ask me again to come with them, but I glared at her until she looked away without saying a word.

So by the time Friday came I was actually eager for the dance to happen. I was done hearing about her primping and was pretty over the weirdness between me and Tyler. No matter what happened, his and Olivia's going to the dance together was going to change things forever. I just hoped it was what she really wanted.

The second the bell rang, Olivia bolted out of the school to meet her mom so they could rush to the salon, leaving me to take my time at my locker.

"Hey," Tyler said, suddenly standing beside me.

"Hi," I said. "Shouldn't you be running home to get ready for the dance too?"

He looked at me funny. "It's like four hours from now."

Right. Only Olivia needed hours to get ready. "So what are you wearing?"

He snorted like it was a ridiculous question. "Pants and a shirt," he said, and then his eyes went wide. "Wait. Why? Should I dress up more than that?"

I slammed my locker and swung my backpack over my shoulder before turning to him. "Probably. She's glamming up."

"Glamming up?"

"Come on," I said, starting to walk toward the door, knowing he'd fall into step beside me. "She's wearing a fancy dress and shoes and is getting her hair and nails done: glamming up."

"Oh."

"What's wrong?" I said, looking at him, not

understanding why it would be a problem that she was making herself *even more* beautiful. For him.

He took a breath and pushed the door open, holding it so I could walk through. "I don't know. I guess I'm nervous."

We walked down the stairs toward the sidewalk. "Why?"

"I . . . Kat, it's *me*. I don't go to dances and *glam up*. I don't even know *how* to dance."

"You don't?" I thought back to the ridiculous quiz and how Olivia was expecting to dance every song with him. Yikes.

He looked at me and shook his head. His face was super red, but honestly, it was the most adorable thing I'd ever seen.

"Can you help me?" he asked. "Show me how to dance?"

"No. I'm not exactly a gazelle. What do I know about dancing?"

He swallowed. "I'm dead."

"No you're not," I said. "Come to my house. Maybe

my mom can help. She used to be a cheerleader."

"That's weird," he said. "Getting your mom to show me how to dance."

"Probably," I agreed. "But less weird than showing up to a dance without being able to dance at all."

He nodded. "Good point."

On one hand, our asking Mom to show Tyler how to dance turned out to be the highlight of her week. On the other, it was totally mortifying for me and Tyler.

Wait, no, not totally mortifying. I mean TOTALLY MORTIFYING.

Of course, the second I told her he needed her help, she jumped up, grabbed her iPhone, and lined up a playlist. After a couple of seconds she led us into the living room and popped her phone into the speaker dock.

"Okay, so let's start with fast dancing," she said as the song began. Perfect—it was a recent 5Style song. Although it wasn't something I would listen to, there was a good chance they'd play it at the dance, and Olivia was definitely going to want to dance to it.

Mom started busting moves right there in the middle of the living room. We just stood there and watched. She actually wasn't bad, moving her feet and hips. She was even smiling like she was enjoying herself, and it seemed to come naturally. Weird.

She waved us over. "Come on, this is a participation thing."

"I'm not going to the dance, so I don't need to learn," I said, dropping onto the couch.

"You still need to learn how to dance, missy. You're going to start getting invited to bat mitzvahs soon," she said. Then, when I groaned and rolled my eyes, she added in her serious *I'm not taking no for an answer* voice, "Let's go, Kat. Now."

Tyler was already at her left side, so with a big sigh I rose and stood to her right. I suddenly hoped Tyler was focused enough on Mom and his own feet that he wouldn't notice that I had zero idea what I was doing. Clearly, I wasn't a gazelle. Nor did I share my mom's dance genes.

"So first you need to get the beat," she said. "Just slide your feet side to side with the music."

I watched what she was doing. While she definitely looked like she was more from the gazelle family than the warthog one, stepping side to side didn't
seem too complicated. I copied her, though I wasn't
sure what to do with my arms, so I just left them at
my sides.

"Don't think too hard," Mom said after a minute.
"Just *feel* the beat."

I *felt* like I was copying her pretty well, but then I
realized maybe she wasn't talking to me, so I peeked
over at Tyler. He had this look on his face like he was
in pain: His forehead was all scrunched up, and his
mouth was open in a grimace. Not his best look, even
with that cute piece of hair hanging in his eyes. Not to
mention that he couldn't seem to find the rhythm of
the music.

Yeah, she was definitely talking to him.

"I . . . I . . . um . . . this is hard," he said, seeming to
struggle with talking and moving his feet (I couldn't
call what he was doing *dancing*).

"Okay, hold on," Mom said as she stopped dancing. "Let's try this. Snap your fingers on the beat." She

started snapping along with the music. I was about to tell her that if Tyler went to the dance and just stood there snapping his fingers, he was asking to be laughed at. Then I realized she was trying to get him to find the beat in a way that was less complicated.

Trying to be encouraging, I started snapping too. I looked at him, hoping he could manage this.

He did. But just barely.

"You hear the music, right?" I asked. Because I couldn't understand how it was such a struggle for him to snap along.

"Yeah," he said, narrowing his eyes at me. "I'm just not good with music. Put a zombie in front of me any day, but this . . . ?" He didn't bother finishing.

"Come on," Mom said, still snapping. "You can do this."

After another twenty minutes and seven songs, it turned out he *couldn't* do it. Not well, anyway, and not for every song. He was getting more and more nervous, so after a quick glance at me, Mom stopped the music.

"Okay, so fast dancing isn't your strong point."

No kidding.

"What about slow dancing?"

Tyler shrugged and blushed. "Won't that be worse?"

Mom shook her head. "Not necessarily. It's slower, and there's not really a beat you have to follow." She went over to her phone and started scrolling. "Let me just find a couple of songs. Kat, get ready."

"What?"

She looked up at me. "He needs to practice with someone."

Huh? "Why can't he practice with you?"

She gave me a look that didn't explain anything but told me she wasn't about to dance with him, then returned to scrolling through her music. "Okay, here are a few."

She started up the first song and then returned to the middle of the floor and grabbed each of us by an arm, tugging us until we were facing each other. I wondered if his face felt as hot as mine did. And if mine looked as red as his was. Probably.

"So there are two ways you can do this," she said, seeming not to notice how horribly embarrassed the kids in front of her were. "The old-fashioned way: Kat, put your left hand on his right shoulder—go on; do this while I'm talking—and Tyler, you put your right hand on her waist. No, a bit higher. There. Now Tyler, you take Kat's right hand with your left and hold them up sort of shoulder height. Good."

Tyler's hand was a bit damp, or maybe mine was, but all I could really think about was that we were holding hands. We'd touched each other before, of course, but that was more like tripping or play punching or trying to knock each other out of the tree that grew between our houses. This was different. We'd never *held hands*.

I wanted to look at him to see if he was feeling as strange and panicky about this as I was, but I couldn't bring myself to meet his eyes. Too weird!

"Okay, now you move," Mom said, breaking into my thoughts.

"Move how?" I asked.

Mom seemed to consider it for a second. "You know what? You're twelve, no need to complicate things. Just sort of go around in circles. Tiny movements with your feet."

"Which way?" Tyler asked.

"It doesn't matter. Say clockwise. Lead forward with your hand that's holding Kat's."

We didn't move.

"Don't be afraid," Mom said, stepping right up to us and getting behind Tyler. She put a hand on his upper arm and the other where his and my hands were joined and sort of nudged. "Just move slowly around. See?"

I felt the toe of Tyler's shoe bump mine, and he muttered, "Sorry."

"It's okay," I said without looking at him.

"You're doing great," Mom said, stepping back away from us. "Now try to relax your shoulders a bit."

I forced my shoulders down and felt Tyler do the same under my hand.

"Now, the most important part," Mom said. "Look at each other and smile. Make sure the person you're dancing with knows you're *not* being tortured."

The way she said it made me laugh, but it was still hard to look into Tyler's eyes. Was dancing always this awkward, or just with him?

"Go on, you two are friends! It's just a dance. You can surely smile at each other."

MOM! I wanted to yell, but I didn't want to let on that I was feeling so weird in case it was just me. Finally, I looked up at him. He kind of did look like he was being tortured. Ugh. I gave him a weak smile that I didn't really feel.

"Good. Now don't forget to keep moving," Mom said.

"Oops," Tyler said, starting to move us around again.

We did almost three turns around until the song ended, and then we let each other go, backing up. Tyler wiped his palms on his jeans, so I did the same.

Mom snorted. "Okay, so the other way—"

"I think he's good," I interrupted, not really wanting to do more even though a new song had come on.

"Kat," she said. "Just chill out, okay? Five more minutes."

It wasn't exactly about the time, but . . . I looked at Tyler, and while he didn't seem eager to do more dancing, he wasn't running away. I exhaled. "Fine."

Mom stepped toward us and put her hand on my back, gently pushing me into Tyler. "Okay, this time, Kat, you put both of your hands on his shoulders, and Tyler, you hold her waist in the same spot, but on both sides. Movement is the same with your feet."

We started moving around in a circle again.

"Good," she said.

This way meant we weren't holding hands, but it felt closer with both of his warm hands on my sides and with our faces lined up more. I sort of *had* to look at him. Well, I looked at his nose, avoiding his eyes at all costs. Though his nose wasn't very interesting, so I looked at his mouth. His lips were pressed together, which I knew meant he was thinking very hard. I focused on a tiny freckle just above his mouth that I'd never noticed before.

"Eyes, kids," Mom said. "Smile. Not torture, remember?"

I swallowed and looked up into Tyler's eyes. He smiled, and I could see the corners of his eyes wrinkle a little.

The phone in the kitchen rang. "Oh, hold on. Keep

going, I'll be right back," Mom said, jogging away.

"Thanks for helping me, Kat," he said once she was gone. He squeezed my waist a bit with his right hand. It made my heart flutter around in my chest.

"No problem," I said, like it was no big deal.

"Sure you don't want to come to the dance?"

I dropped my eyes from his. "No. I'd just be in the way."

"No you wouldn't. I promise."

"It's okay," I said. "I don't really want to go."

"Okay," he said. "But if you change your mind . . ."

Suddenly there was a flash. With a gasp I turned and saw my mother standing there in the hall holding a camera aimed at us. "You did *NOT* just take a picture!"

"Of course I did. You two are *adorable*."

Which signaled the end of our dancing lesson.

Chapter 14

DAD CALLED AND TOLD MOM THAT WE SHOULDN'T wait for him, so at dinner it was just her, Laura, and me. I was still a bit weirded out about the whole dancing thing, but was trying to get over it and make myself feel better by thinking about all the time I had to devote to my manga this weekend.

The only sounds around the table were from eating: forks on plates, a glass being set down, the squeak of Laura's chair as she shook salt out of the shaker onto her food, the sucking squirt of the ketchup bottle as I drew a squiggly red line across my shepherd's pie.

No one was talking, but it didn't bother me, since

in my head I was trying to figure out my next illustration for *Hector: Ninja Cat*.

Suddenly Mom broke into my thoughts. "Are you sure you don't want to go to that dance, sweetie?"

Sigh. "Very sure," I answered, snapping the cap closed on the ketchup.

"But Tyler is going."

"I know that," I said, digging my fork into my shepherd's pie and shoveling the heaping load of food into my mouth.

"Pig," Laura said.

I glared at her, but it wasn't like I could say anything, since my mouth was completely full.

"Laura," Mom warned before turning back to me. "I don't understand why you don't want to go if Tyler is going."

I sighed as I chewed, trying to figure out what to say.

"He's going with Olivia," Laura said. "Isn't he?"

"Oh," Mom said, her serious tone making me look up at her. "I'm sorry, honey."

"Sorry for what?" I asked.

Mom looked at Laura and then back to me.

"Well . . . he's your friend, and I thought . . ."

I stared at the red mess on my plate. "There's nothing to think. They're going to the dance together and I'm not."

"You *should* go," Laura said. I thought she was making fun of me, but when I looked at her, she wasn't laughing or even smirking. "You should. Olivia and Tyler aren't right for each other."

"Opposites attract," I said, using Olivia's words, even though I didn't totally believe them. Still, Tyler had asked her to go, so he obviously liked her.

"Whatever. You should go."

"I have nothing to wear."

"You can wear my blue dress," Laura said. "I'm sure it would fit you."

"No thanks," I said.

"Kat," Mom started, but before she could go any further, I pushed my chair back from the table.

"Can I please be excused?"

"Kat, we're not trying to upset you," Mom said. "We just don't want you to miss out. If your friends are there—"

"May I *please* be excused?" I asked again, hoping I could get away from the table before I started crying. Because my throat was getting tight, and I knew tears were seconds away.

Mom exhaled. "Yes, you may. But Kitty-Kat—"

Her using my old nickname made me feel even more like a baby, and I already felt stupid enough. "No! I don't want to go to the dance, okay? That's the end of it!"

She might have said something else after that, but I couldn't tell, because I ran away from the table and up to my room, where I slammed the door behind me. I cringed at how loud it was and figured I was probably going to get in trouble, but whatever. Laura slammed her door pretty much eighty times a day for no reason at all. Now it was my turn.

I sure felt like I had plenty of reasons, although the last thing I was going to do was explain to them that going to the dance meant I would have a front-row seat to watch Tyler dancing with Olivia.

Which meant he would *not* be dancing with me.

Chapter 15

AFTER A WHILE, I SNUCK OUT OF MY ROOM AND downstairs to get a glass of milk. Not only was I thirsty, but if I had to see one more texted picture of Olivia's hair, Olivia's nails, Olivia's dress, Olivia's shiny, glossed lips, I was going to scream. I needed a distraction.

Mom was sitting at the kitchen table and looked up as I came into the room. "Honey, I'm sorry about before," she said. "I didn't mean to push you."

I shrugged. "I don't want to talk about it."

"That's fine. I understand. . . ." She trailed off. She

sounded like she wanted to say more, but she didn't, so I poured the milk.

"What are your plans for tonight?" she asked.

"I was going to work on my manga."

"Why don't you take a break? Let's watch TV, make popcorn."

I didn't really want to, but the look on her face told me she did. Dad still wasn't home, and Laura was up in her room, so Mom was probably lonely.

"Okay," I said. "But please, no more questions about the dance."

"Deal."

We had just started an episode of *Dancing with the Stars* that Mom had on the DVR when I got a text. It could only be from either Tyler or Olivia. I glanced at the clock: It was seven minutes after seven, which meant the dance had started seven minutes ago.

I sighed, not wanting to deal with the drama. I tried to ignore it, but the texts kept coming and my phone kept beeping. Mom exhaled loudly in a way that let me know she wasn't going to tolerate many more before she said something. I slid my phone out of my pocket, and it only took one glance of the many texts in all caps to see that Olivia was having a meltdown. A *major* meltdown.

I didn't even get a chance to read one text before the phone rang.

I jumped off the couch and went into the hall to answer.

"Hel—"

"KAT!" Olivia practically screamed into the phone.

I took a breath because I knew what was coming. "Livvy, what's going on?"

"It's going *awful*. You have to get here and help me!"

I was about to ask her where she was, but then I heard a flush, telling me she was hiding out in the bathroom.

"Olivia, we've been through this. Calm down and tell me what's going on."

"Okay, so my whole plan was to dance with him so we wouldn't have to talk, but Kat, *he won't dance with me*! He just wants to sit on the bleachers and talk about those dumb books."

I sighed, hoping my shattered eardrums would heal someday. "What do you mean he won't dance?" I asked, but I was just buying myself time, because I knew what had happened. He'd realized he couldn't dance and figured he'd be safer on the bleachers. "Even slow songs?"

"There haven't been any yet."

"Well, why don't you just talk to him about the books during the fast songs and then slow-dance with him? Compromise, you know."

"Kat, I *can't* talk to him about the books. I haven't read any more of the first one. I have the cards you made in my purse, but I can't exactly look at those while I'm talking to him."

I sighed. "Do you want to do the phone thing?"

"My hair is in an updo—there's nowhere to hide the earbuds!"

Right. I'd forgotten about that detail. "Livvy, I'm sorry. I can't help you." I felt bad, but what could I do? She had asked for this.

"Yes you can. You *can* help me; you just *won't*."

Ouch. That made me mad. After all, I had done

everything—and I mean *everything*—I could to help her already. I took a deep breath to try to not freak out. "Olivia—"

"Please, Kat. *Please.* I'm so messing this up, and I know you can help me if you just come to the dance. Please. I'll do anything you want. I'll even find a guy for you to dance with. TJ is here and he looks really cute and he—"

"Livvy!" I interrupted. "I'm not coming to the dance. I have told you a million times that I don't like TJ!"

As I was saying this, a text came through. It was from Tyler. My heart pounded, because for half a second I thought of the teeny, tiny possibility that he was texting me to tell me he wished I was there. I took a moment to read the text.

Tyler: *Olivia is hiding in the bathroom. What a mess. I screwed this up so bad. Kat? What do I do?*

My heart sank. He didn't want me to come. He wanted me to help him with Olivia.

I took a deep breath. I thought about how I needed to get over my crush once and for all. That meant getting them together, no matter what it took. Even if it meant going to that dance.

"Livvy?" I said into my phone.

"Yeah?"

"I'll be there as soon as I can."

Chapter 16

I ENDED THE CALL AND LOOKED UP TO SEE LAURA standing right there. "Gah!" I exclaimed, pressing my hand to my heart. "You freaked me out!"

She grabbed my other arm and tugged me toward the stairs that led up to our bedrooms. "Come with me."

I was going that way because I needed to change, so I let her drag me along. "What for? I need to get out of my sweats."

She looked over her shoulder at me. "I know. I heard your part of the conversation. And I'm going to help you."

"Why? I just need to change my clothes. I have to get there right away!"

Laura squeezed my arm—not enough for it to hurt, but enough that I knew she meant business. "Not before I help you."

"Why are you so interested in helping me?" I asked.

She frowned like it should be obvious. "You're my sister."

"So? That doesn't stop you from being mean to me all the time." I pulled my arm from her grasp.

"I'm not mean to you."

I gave her an *Oh, really?* look. "You're crabby to everyone."

She exhaled and looked over my head toward where Mom sat in the living room. "Just let me help you, okay? I don't mean to be crabby; just school is really hard this year. It's stressful, okay? It's not about you."

"Is that why the lunches you make are so awful?"

"What?" She frowned. "Awful?"

"You don't cut my apple, and the sandwiches are always a mess."

Laura sighed and closed her eyes for a second. "Mornings are the worst. Honestly, I'm not trying to make your lunches awful on purpose."

My throat got really tight. "I thought you hated me for some reason."

"What?" She put her arm around me and squeezed. "Of course not. I love you, little Kitty-Kat. I just . . . ninth grade is *really* hard. It's such a big, confusing building, and I have so many teachers and classes. And with Candace gone this year . . ." She took a deep breath, and I could tell she was getting upset, which made me sad for her. She exhaled loudly. "I have a lot going on, that's all."

I thought about that. In a way, I understood. I mean, I was terrified of high school, and I had only just started seventh grade! And one of her best friends had moved away over the summer, which had to make it even harder. Still . . . "You could be nicer to me," I said. "And to Mom and Dad."

"I am trying to be nice to you *right now*, but you're not making it easy," she said, giving me a very wide-eyed look.

"Fine. But no makeup."

"*Some* makeup," she corrected me. She took my arm again—more gently this time—and led me up to her room. "You're going to a dance, not a tractor pull."

"Fine," I relented. "A *tiny bit* of makeup. And I don't even know what a tractor pull is."

"Never mind. Let's get you ready."

"Okay," I said. "But about the other stuff. How about I talk to Mom and Dad? Maybe I can make our lunches from now on."

She stopped and dropped my arm, looking at me. "You'd do that?"

I nodded. "I'm sure I can handle it. I mean, I'm not a baby. And that way you don't have to stress about it or get up so early, and I get what I want for lunch."

My big sister threw her arms around me. "That would be awesome."

I hugged her back for a second but remembered Olivia and how frantic she'd been on the phone. "Okay, come on, we'd better do this."

*

"Oh, Kat!" Mom exclaimed, jumping up off the couch when I came back downstairs fifteen minutes later. I was dressed in Laura's royal blue dress that she had worn to her eighth-grade graduation. It was plain enough that I didn't feel totally ridiculous, but still looked a little glam. It was sleeveless and velvety on top with lace on the skirt—a bit too girly for my liking, but when I'd looked in the mirror, I'd been secretly happy with the reflection staring back at me. Not that I'd admit it to anyone.

Thanks to Laura, I was also lightly makeupped (just brown mascara and a tiny bit of liner to make my eyes stand out under my glasses) and lip-glossed (light pink and shiny).

Mom looked from me and then to Laura and back. "Does this mean you're going to the dance?"

I couldn't exactly tell her *why* I needed to go, but it didn't matter, because obviously she was excited. That meant she would drive me. "Yes. For a little while. You can pick me up at eight thirty."

"You look beautiful," she said. "Laura, you were

right; that dress does look great on her. And the shoes . . ."

Thankfully, the sparkly silver ballet flats didn't have heels. I didn't think there would be any chance I *wouldn't* fall down if I had to walk in high heels.

"We have to go," I said. "My friends are waiting for me."

"I'll go get my keys," Mom said, hurrying past me toward the kitchen.

I turned to my sister. "Thanks for this," I said with a grin. "You're not such a horrible big sister after all."

"You aren't such a bratty *little* sister either," she said, but she was smiling. She leaned toward me and tucked a piece of hair into the fancy-looking ponytail she'd done. It had only taken her a minute to put it all up, but it looked really good. "You look awesome, Kat."

"Thanks to you."

"And a little makeup." She smirked.

Mom came back from the kitchen with her phone in her hand. "I need a picture."

"No, Mom," I said, holding my hand in front of my face. "I have to get there!"

She put her hand on her hip. "I'm not driving you until I get one. So we can do this the easy way or the time-consuming way."

"Fine, but hurry up!"

Laura snickered but stood back so Mom had a clear shot of me.

I stuck out my tongue, but Mom laughed and took the picture anyway. Then I remembered when we'd been upstairs and Laura had turned me around to see my dressed-up self in the mirror. I'd been shocked at how good I looked. Maybe a picture wasn't a bad idea.

"Okay," I said. "Take another one."

Mom nodded, and instead of sticking out my tongue, this time I smiled when she aimed her phone at me.

We were almost out the door when my sister said my name. I turned and looked at her. "Yeah?"

"Go get him," she said with a wink.

All I could do was stare at my sister, because no words would come. I knew what she meant, but I was only going to the dance to help my friend. Well, technically, *both* my friends. Even if there had ever been even the teeny-tiniest chance that Tyler might like me, it was way too late to do anything about it now. He and Olivia were basically a couple. Tonight would clinch it; I was only going to the dance to make sure it happened. That was the only reason: for my friends.

So I told myself in my head. Loudly.

"Come on, Kat," Mom said, putting her hand on my shoulder to guide me out the door.

Chapter 17

I WALKED INTO THE GYM BUT STAYED IN THE shadows near the door, scanning the room to see if I could find Olivia and Tyler. There were groups of kids standing around the perimeter, and some were sitting up on the bleachers. Loud music was playing—a fast song—but not many kids were dancing. In fact there was just one group of five girls on the dance floor. I could see right away (thanks to her being so tall) that Olivia was among them, along with Jasmine and Zoe.

They all looked really comfortable on the dance floor. Like a herd of gazelles who probably didn't have to get their moms to teach them how to dance.

Another eye sweep of the room and I noticed Tyler sitting by himself on the bleachers, looking really unhappy as he watched Olivia. Poor guy. But as I was watching him and trying to figure out what to do, he stood up and started to walk to the side of the bleachers, toward the stairs. I ducked deeper into the shadows, suddenly not wanting him to see me.

He came down to the gym floor and almost passed me. He took one last look at Olivia and then headed out into the hallway. I sidestepped over to the doorway and peeked out just in time to see him turn in to the boys' bathroom. I rushed over to Olivia.

"Kat!" she squealed, right before she threw her arms around me. "I'm so glad you're here."

She made way for Zoe and Jasmine to give me hugs too, but I quickly pulled away from them: I was there to do a job and didn't have a lot of time.

"I just saw him go to the bathroom," I said. "Why was he sitting by himself?"

She glanced at the group of girls and then back at me. "Because he didn't want to dance."

"But he's your date."

She frowned. "But this is a *dance*. And it's not like I can talk to him . . ."

I grabbed her hand and pulled her away from the other girls. "So how are we going to fix this?"

She just stared at me.

"Livvy?"

"What?"

"You said you wanted me to help you. I'm here to help you. What are we supposed to do?"

"I . . . I don't know," she said. "I guess I never really thought that far ahead."

I rolled my eyes, then looked around the gym, hoping the answer would just pop into my brain, when a slow song came on. My heart lurched as I thought about slow-dancing with Tyler in my living room.

Olivia squealed. "OMG! This is 5Style's new song. I *need* to dance!"

"Tyler is still in the bathroom," I pointed out.

Her face fell.

I heard my name from behind me and turned to find myself face to face with TJ Stevens. He was standing there with his hands in his pockets looking kind of nervous.

"Oh, hey," I said, guessing what he was doing. "You can't dance with Olivia; she's here with Tyler."

His eyes darted over to Olivia and then back at me. "Uh . . . actually, I was going to ask *you* to dance," he said.

What? My face got hot as I realized Olivia had to be behind this. "Oh . . . uh . . . I . . ."

Suddenly I was pushed from behind and almost bashed into TJ. Managing to stop myself just in time, I whipped around and adjusted my glasses before I glared at the person who was *supposed* to be my best cousin. She didn't look sorry. Instead she was standing there, giving me a pointed look that seemed to scream, *Go dance with him!*

But I wasn't there to dance; I was there to help her. "Thanks, TJ," I said. "But, um, no thanks."

"Oh. Okay. Well, I'll see you later then, I guess."

He pretty much ran away. I felt bad, but it wasn't like I could have danced with him anyway.

"You should have danced with him, Kat!" Olivia scolded from behind me. "Why didn't you?"

"Because I'm only here to help you! For the millionth time, *I do not like him,*" I half yelled at her, really losing my patience.

The smile disappeared from her face.

I took her arm and tugged her over to the side of the bleachers. "You need to spend time with Tyler. He's not a very good dancer, and he doesn't feel comfortable, so you're going to have to figure out how to talk to him."

"But I tried that. I can't," she whined.

I glanced over toward the bleachers and had a sudden idea. "Why don't you sit with him up there and I'll hide underneath and help you?"

She followed my eyes to the benches, and her face lit up. "Oh. So he won't see you but I'll be able to hear you."

"Yeah. But don't go too high up or you won't be able to hear me over the music."

"Okay, yeah, that will work, Kat."

"But Livvy?" I said, stopping to say one last thing before I ducked under the bleachers.

"What?"

"This is the last time. I can't keep doing this, okay?"

I held my breath, waiting for her answer.

She looked mad at first, but she sighed and then nodded. "I guess you're right. Let's make tonight go perfect, and then he and I will be official."

And then what? I didn't say; I just nodded and disappeared under the bleachers. I waited to see her thin ankles and teetering heels so I could position myself underneath them.

It wasn't long before I heard the metallic thumping as she and Tyler made their way down the third row. The second would have been better, as the third one took them farther up and away from me, but it wasn't like I could tell her to change places now. The benches creaked as they sat down, giving me full view of their feet and ankles but not much else. I could hear them talking, but not very well over the music.

I lightly touched Olivia's ankle and whispered, "Talk louder."

"Sorry, Tyler, the music is really loud. What did you say?" she almost yelled.

"I asked if you liked the DVDs I lent you," he

responded, not quite as loudly but loud enough that I could hear.

"Oh, yes, I did!" she said. "Especially the third one."

"That one is my favorite, too!" he said. "What did you think of the fight scene?"

"What did I think of the fight scene?" she repeated as she tapped her foot, and I knew that meant I was supposed to help. But I hadn't seen them! He'd lent the DVDs to her before me!

"I haven't seen them," I whispered up to her.

Just then Tyler shifted, making the bench creak.

"What are you doing?" Olivia screeched.

"I thought I heard something," Tyler said. "Like a voice. Is there someone under the bleachers?"

I jumped back into the shadows, my heart thudding against my ribs.

"Of course not! Why would there be?" Olivia blurted. She quickly changed the subject back to the DVDs. "The fight scene. Right. I thought it was awesome. That was my favorite part."

"You didn't think it was a bit much?"

"Uhhhh," she said, tapping her foot frantically.

I edged closer, getting as close to Olivia as I could, "Tell him you thought it fit the story," I suggested.

Tyler shifted again, but I ducked back away. This was ridiculous! We were going to get so busted.

"I mean, yeah, maybe it was a bit much, but it fit the story."

"I guess. But that whole baby thing, right?"

Olivia's toe tapped like crazy.

Baby thing? I had nothing. "I don't know!" I whispered.

"Yeah, the baby thing," Olivia said. "That was . . . amazing!"

There was a long silence, and I would have given anything to know what Tyler was thinking. Also: What the heck was the baby thing?

"Anyway," Olivia said. "I'm having such a good time. I like your tie."

Tie? He's wearing a tie? I hadn't noticed before, and I didn't even know he *owned* a tie. I tried to angle myself so I could see up, but it was no use; he was hidden by the bench and the supports of the bleachers.

"Thanks," he said. "You look . . . pretty."

"I know, right? I got my hair done and everything."

I rolled my eyes. Subtle, Livvy.

"So . . . uh . . . ," Tyler said. "Since we're here together and we have so much in common and obviously we like the same things and all, I was thinking . . ."

I angled myself closer so I could hear, and when I twisted my head just right and looked up, I could see a sliver of each of them through the gap.

"Yeah?" Olivia asked, though I could barely hear it over the music.

"I . . . um . . . I just really like you, Livvy."

Even though I guess I knew it was coming, I gasped a little and then held my breath as I waited for her answer.

Tyler moved again, and I jumped away, pressing my back against the wall, making myself as small as I could. "Okay, I'm sure I heard something that time!" he said.

"It's nothing!" Olivia said. "What were you saying? It sounded like something REALLY important."

He shifted toward her, and I edged closer to hear, even though I didn't really want to. "I . . . I, um, wanted to know if you like me, too."

"Yes," she said without hesitation.

"Oh. That's great," he said, sounding a little out of breath. Just as the song ended and a silence fell over the gym, there was a slow creak from the bleachers as Tyler leaned toward her, and I could see through the opening as his hand crept forward toward hers.

My heart felt like it broke into pieces right then. They were going to hold hands! I had to force myself not to run out of the gym. Now that they were pretty much official, the last thing I wanted was for him to see me at the dance, no matter how nice I looked.

I was thinking about how best to sneak out when . . .

THBBBFFFBBBTTTT!!!!

A loud fart noise sounded from beside me, scaring me half to death!

"Gah!" I yelled out before I even realized what was happening. Then I heard a bunch of giggles and turned to see that I wasn't alone under the bleachers—there were a couple of totally immature sixth graders with one of those rubber farting balloons!

"You little stinkers!" I hissed at them, but then I had bigger problems. There were loud, banging footsteps on the bleachers, and before I could even think of what to do or where to go, Tyler was peering at me from the end of the bleachers.

"Kat?" he said, a confused look on his face as he looked me up and down. "What are you doing here? And why are you under the bleachers?"

"Oh, uh," I looked around at the floor. "I just got here and I lost one of my earrings and thought maybe it rolled under here."

Olivia showed up beside him just then, all wide-eyed and panicky.

"Maybe I can help you find it," Tyler said. He crept down under the bleachers toward me and looked around, thankfully not noticing I wasn't even wearing earrings.

Olivia followed him. She and I exchanged glances, but it wasn't like we could read each other's minds exactly, so there wasn't much I could do other than shrug. Plus, I had no idea what to do. Bolting out of the gym seemed like a pretty good idea at that moment, though.

"Oh, you lost your lip gloss?" Olivia said suddenly.

I glanced at her and she was rummaging through her purse and then threw a tube on the floor before pointing at it and yelling out, "There it is!"

Uh-oh! Worse than her saying the wrong thing was that the tube of lip gloss wasn't all that came out of her purse. Right there, up against Tyler's foot, were two of the cheat-sheet cards. They must have fallen out with the lip gloss and sailed right over to him, like magnets that knew they were all about him.

"You dropped something," he said as he bent down to pick them up. "What's this?"

I was frozen to the spot for half a second and then dove for the cards in his hand, except his zombie-slashing, lightning-fast reflexes kicked in, and he pulled the cards out of my reach before I could grab them.

I glanced at Olivia, whose face looked like she was watching a horror movie. Mine probably looked the same.

"What the . . . ?" Tyler said. His voice wasn't curious anymore. It was confused and maybe a little bit mad. Then he looked up at me and Olivia. "My favorite foods, color, sports? Plot of *Knights at Sunrise*? I don't understand. What *is* this?" he asked as he held up the second card and turned it over.

Olivia's face was frozen, so she was obviously no help, but all I could do was stutter at Tyler.

"Is this some sort of joke?" he asked, and I could tell he wasn't just a little bit mad. He was *a lot* mad. "You guys tricked me?"

I wanted to say no, but I couldn't lie to him when he was staring at me like that, hurt and anger in his eyes. I couldn't even look at him. I dropped my eyes to my hands. "Tyler, I . . ."

But while I was trying to find the words to explain, he said, "I can't believe this." Then he was gone, out from under the bleachers.

I followed him and looked up in time to see the back of him running into the hall.

"Tyler!" I yelled, but he didn't stop.

I looked at Olivia.

"Now what are we supposed to do?" she asked.

I didn't even respond. I just ran out into the hall to try to catch him.

Chapter 18

I DIDN'T HAVE TO RUN FAR (GOOD THING, SINCE running in a formal dress and ballet flats isn't exactly like running in sneakers) because Tyler was sitting on the concrete steps just outside the school doors.

"Tyler," I said, ignoring the cool autumn wind that seemed to blow right through my dress.

His shoulders stiffened, but he didn't say anything. Instead he stood up and started walking away from me.

I panicked. "Tyler, wait."

He stopped and folded his arms but didn't turn toward me, which really hurt. But of course the way he was acting was all my fault. Well, Olivia's, too. But

I'd known the whole time that it was a bad plan, and I'd still gone along with it. I hurried around him so we faced each other, but he still wouldn't look at me.

"I'm so sorry," I said, my voice cracking.

Finally he looked at me, anger all over his face. "For what? For tricking me or because I found out?"

"I never meant to trick you," I said.

His eyebrows went up on his forehead as he snorted. "Really? You hid under the bleachers to feed Olivia lines . . . you wrote a *cheat sheet* about me—don't deny it, I know your handwriting—and you *weren't* trying to trick me?"

"Well . . . uh . . ."

He glared at me, making me fidget and shift my weight from foot to foot.

"How many times, Kat?"

"How many times what?"

"How many times did you and her fool me, make me think she liked all the same things I do? Into thinking she was interested in me?"

"She *is* interested in you," I said, almost choking on the words. "That part is real!"

"I thought we were friends, Kat," he said. *"Best* friends. We've known each other forever, and I thought . . ." He rubbed his forehead and then looked back up at me. "Why? Why would you do this?"

"Because . . ." *I knew you wouldn't like me.* "Because you and Olivia belong together," I blurted out. "You just didn't see it."

He shook his head. "What makes you think that? We have *nothing* in common. Like, absolutely nothing—I *knew* that, but then . . . Why did you trick me into thinking we did?"

"She's beautiful and on the dance team and is fun and popular, and I thought . . ." My voice fizzled out because my throat was so dry and I was suddenly just tired of faking it. All I wanted was for all this to be over and to have my friend back, but now I'd gone and messed everything up. Probably even forever.

"You think I care about those things? You think I would like someone just because they're pretty and popular?" The anger in his eyes turned to hurt. That was worse than anything. I wished the ground would open up and swallow me whole so I wouldn't have to see how bad I'd made him feel. But the earth below me was solid, and Tyler wasn't done with me yet.

"Is that what you think of me, Kat? Because that is worse than the lies!"

I could barely breathe. My tongue was frozen in my mouth, but even if I had been able to speak, I wouldn't have known what to say. I was the worst friend ever. All I could do was stand there and try my hardest not to cry, but there was no stopping the tears that were filling my eyes. I couldn't even bring myself to stop him when he started to walk away from me.

But after just two steps he stopped and turned back toward me, holding up the cheat sheet that was still in his hand. "By the way, you got one thing wrong."

I swallowed and managed to croak out one word: "What?"

"My favorite thing isn't playing Zombie Slashers," he said. "My favorite thing *was* playing Zombie Slashers with my best friend. *You*, Kat."

The tears rushed out then, and I tried to swipe them away.

"It was you playing that day on Xbox, wasn't it?"

I nodded.

Looking away from me, he let out one of those dry laughs that have nothing to do with anything funny and shook his head. "I should have known she would never be that good."

Without another word he turned again and walked off, leaving me standing on the school steps.

I knew I should go inside to talk to Olivia, but my brain was tired and sad, and I just wanted to go home, crawl into bed, and sleep for a week. Then I'd deal with the mess I'd made.

But first I needed to get home. I knew I should probably call Mom to come pick me up earlier than I'd told her, but I didn't want to explain why I was leaving the dance already. And even though she'd been nice to me earlier, Laura would probably just laugh about how badly I'd messed things up if I came home early.

So I decided to just walk the few blocks home and get there just before Mom was set to leave. There was only one problem with that: Tyler lived right next door to me. Which meant I was going to have to go right past his house, unless I took the long way and came to my house from the other direction. That wasn't a bad idea, since Tyler was walking home too; the last thing I wanted to do was run into him now that he hated my guts.

I gave the school doors one last glance, a little hurt that Olivia hadn't come to make sure I was okay. But maybe she was hiding in the bathroom or something. If that was the case, I was being just as bad a friend by not seeking her out, but I still couldn't bring myself to go back inside.

With a heavy sigh I started down the stairs and headed home.

When I finally got there, both cars were in the driveway and the lights were on in the living room. I couldn't face my family and pretend I wasn't devastated. Not yet. I walked around the back of the house and up to the tree between my house and Tyler's. For a second I considered climbing it right up to Tyler's bedroom window, but I wasn't going to do that now, not after what had happened, and especially not in a dress. I hadn't done it in a while—not since our last scavenger hunt.

I looked up at the window and watched as the light went on in his room, making me back up against the tree, but I knew he wouldn't look out the window anyway. I tucked the dress under me and sat down on one of the gnarly roots, folding my arms up against the chill, which still kind of felt good in a weird way.

"I have to fix this," I said aloud to myself. I tried to think up a plan, but then I realized that plans were what had gotten me into this mess.

It was time to tell everyone the truth. No matter how hard that might be.

Coming clean to Olivia felt like it would be slightly less hard than doing the same with Tyler, so I'd start with her first.

Chapter 19

AFTER A WHILE I GOT SO COLD SITTING OUT ON
the tree that I started to shiver and realized there was
no putting it off any longer; I had to go inside my
house.

I went around to the front porch and entered the
code to unlock the door, which meant there was no
sneaking past my parents, because the buttons beep
when you press them.

"Kat?" Mom called out, but then she met me in the
hallway. I could hear Dad snoring in the living room,
so she'd probably come out to talk to me without wak-
ing him. "What are you doing home already? I was

going to leave soon to come get you. Is everything okay?"

I pasted a smile on my face. "Yes, everything's fine. I was just tired, that's all."

She frowned. "How did you get home?"

Uh-oh. "I walked."

"With Tyler?"

She was staring at me so intently that I couldn't lie to her even though I was about to get in trouble. "No, he left earlier."

She folded her arms across her chest. "So you walked home by yourself in the dark."

I nodded.

"Why didn't you call me?"

Because I was embarrassed. Because I didn't want to explain. Because I wasn't thinking about how I'm not supposed to walk alone after dark.

I just shrugged.

Mom exhaled and then hugged me, which was weird, because she was obviously mad. "Go upstairs and get changed while I talk to your father about this."

My father let out a huge snore at that moment.

Mom and I both laughed, but then her face tightened and she said, "You're still in trouble, missy. Go on. I need to wake up the ogre in the other room."

Without another word I headed up the stairs. I heard music coming from Laura's room, so I snuck past and slipped through my door, closing it quietly behind me. The last thing I wanted to do was to have to explain to her how horribly things had gone at the dance.

After I changed out of the dress and into my pajamas, I got my phone out of my purse and held my breath, hoping there would be messages from Olivia and Tyler.

Half my hopes came true when I saw several from Olivia asking where I was and what had happened to Tyler. Trying not to focus on the fact that there was nothing from Tyler, I texted Olivia back.

Kat: *Sorry. Home now. Tyler left—was pretty mad.*

Olivia: *at me, too?*

What? How could she even ask that? Of course he was mad at *both* of us.

Kat: *yes.*

Olivia: ☹

Kat: *Can I come over tomorrow?*

I chewed on my thumbnail as I waited for her return text.

Olivia: *sure. I'll text you in the am. Gotta go! They're playing 5Style!*

I stared at my phone for a few minutes. Okay, so obviously she wasn't as upset about the whole Tyler thing as I was. She actually didn't seem upset about it at all and had stayed at the dance. Did she even really like him? Or was it just that he'd gotten cute over the summer? The more I thought about how she'd been acting while we were trying to get him to like her, the more I realized she'd called pretty much everything that Tyler likes (which is pretty much everything *I* like) boring: *Knights at Sunrise*, the samurai movies, Zombie Slashers, manga.

Not only did she think all those things were boring, but she didn't even seem to care enough about Tyler to give them a chance. I'd always known that she and I didn't have very much in common, but this year it seemed even worse. She was into makeup and dance, and I was getting more interested in stuff she didn't even care to understand. But we were family, and there were a lot of things to love about her.

But when it came to her and Tyler, how could they be together if she only cared about what he looked like? Or what other girls thought? Or if everything he thought about her was based on a big, fat lie?

Thinking all this just made me feel a thousand times worse for tricking him into thinking he liked her when, really, the person he thought he liked was . . . me.

Me.

Plain old Kat the warthog who could barely dance. Who is short and has braces and glasses. But who loves manga and has read every single Blackwood Knights book at least three times. Who can kick Tyler's butt at Zombie Slashers. Kat, the girl who Tyler had said was no less pretty than Olivia.

My heart fluttered in my chest as I connected the dots, as Dad liked to say. Maybe Tyler really *could* like me. The cute boy next door who was so much more than just a cute boy. My cute best friend.

I just had to figure out how to get him back.

Chapter 20

"I CAN'T STAY LONG," I SAID AS OLIVIA AND I WALKED into her bedroom the next morning. She closed the door so it was just her and me. Oh, and all the boys from 5Style, thanks to the millions of posters all over her walls. "I'm grounded, so I had to tell my parents I'd already promised to help you with our English home-work. I don't think they bought it—they only gave me a half hour, and that includes the time it takes to walk here and home. Honestly, if we weren't related, I don't think they would have let me out at all."

"Grounded?" Olivia asked. "For what?"

"Walking home by myself in the dark last night."

She cringed as she sat down on her bed. "That's sort of my fault for dragging you to the dance. I'm sorry."

I sat on her bed and scooted up beside her against the headboard. I shook my head. "No. It was my decision to walk home alone. I should have called my mom. I was . . . I wasn't really thinking straight at the time."

"Right. Because of Tyler."

I nodded as I looked down at my hands and took a deep breath, determined not to get all teary about it.

"So what happened?"

I shrugged. "He was really mad."

"Still?"

"Yeah. I mean, I haven't talked to him yet, but I'm pretty sure he's still mad." My silent phone pretty much guaranteed it. I hadn't gotten the guts to text him yet, but I would after I straightened things out with Olivia.

"Wait . . . ," Olivia said in a tone that made me look up at her. "Do you . . . do you *like* him?"

My first instinct was to lie about it, but look where all the lying had gotten me. Plus, I could feel my face heating up like crazy, so there wasn't much point when my red cheeks would give me away. "I think so."

"Kat!" she scolded, her eyes wide. "Why didn't you *tell* me?"

Wasn't it obvious why? "Because *you* liked him!"

"So?" She snorted like *I* was the one who was being ridiculous. "I wasn't *totally in love* with him or anything. It's not like he's one of the members of 5Style!" She waved around her room at the posters.

You have got to be kidding me, I thought. "Livvy, I thought you *really* liked him."

She cringed. "I mean, he's totally cute, but you were right; he's probably not my type. He's *way* more your type. I can't believe you never said anything. If you had put him on that quiz instead of your dumb cat, none of this would have happened!"

I wasn't sure whether to hug her or clobber her. "I guess I thought he'd pick you over me."

She tilted her head and frowned. "Why? Because I'm horrible at math and don't read? I'm sure that's *exactly* what he's looking for, not the cute girl who knows what cookies he likes and can quote his favorite books because they're *her* favorite books too."

I couldn't help but smile. "I was stupid."

"Normally you're not, but this time you were, Kat. Plus, you should have told me! You should *never*, *ever* lie to your best cousin."

"You're totally right. I never should have lied," I said, not just thinking of her.

"Although, I guess we shouldn't have lied to Tyler, either, huh?" she said.

"No," I said. "We shouldn't have."

"How are you going to fix it with him?"

"I don't know," I said.

"We'll figure it out," she said in a very take-charge voice.

I got up off her bed. "Thanks, but I need to figure this out on my own."

"You're not the only one who screwed up, Kat," she said, coming to stand beside me. "I owe him an apology too."

I nodded, then checked my phone for the time. "I should go."

"By the way," she said as I turned toward the door, "you looked really pretty last night. I'm not just saying that because you're my best cousin, either. You really did."

Letting go of the door handle, I gave her a hug. "Thanks, Livvy. You did too."

She squeezed me tight. "Thanks."

I pulled away. "We good?"

"Always."

"And you're sure you don't mind if me and Tyler . . ."

She waved me off. "No. You and him make a lot more sense. Plus . . ." She got this goofy smile on her face and started fidgeting on her feet.

"What?" I asked, knowing she had something to tell me.

"After you left last night? TJ came over and asked me to dance. Turns out he loves 5Style and is an amazing dancer. He's SO cute, don't you think?"

I couldn't help but laugh. "He's totally cute—you know, *for you*. I'm really happy for you, Livvy," I said, meaning it.

She gave me a big smile that told me what she'd said was true: We would *always* be good, no matter what. After all, we were best cousins.

"Okay, I'd better go." I pulled her bedroom door open. "Oh, and about tomorrow . . ."

Olivia frowned and cocked her head to the side. "Tomorrow?"

"Volunteering at the shelter?"

She laughed and waved her hand at me. "Oh, that. Yeah, I'm totally quitting. Sorry."

I rolled my eyes. "I figured."

She walked me down to the front door. "Good luck with Tyler."

I nodded, knowing I was going to need it.

I texted him a bunch of messages telling him I was sorry.

He ignored me.

I texted him jokes.

He ignored me some more.

I texted him a picture of my Xbox controller with a question mark (even though I couldn't actually play, since I was grounded, but . . .).

Nothing.

Every text that he didn't return hurt more and more.

Saturday night, I tried one last thing.

Kat: *Don't forget Dad's driving us to the shelter tomorrow. Come over at 9:30*

Finally, he texted me back.

Tyler: *I'm taking the bus.*

Yep, that one hurt the most. Would he ever forgive me?

The next morning I was a huge bundle of nerves as I got ready to go to the shelter. My stomach was so tense, I could barely eat my breakfast. What I did manage to eat (a slice of toast with peanut butter) sat like a rock in my gut. Even my stomach was angry at me!

Finally, at nine o'clock, I planted myself in a chair in my living room, positioning myself so I could see the edge of Tyler's front porch through a gap in the curtains. If he left, I'd see him, and if he didn't, well, maybe he would drive with us after all.

At twenty-two minutes after, Dad hollered my name from the hallway.

"I'm right here," I said.

"Oh," he said, lowering his voice. "Ready to go?"

I glanced down at my phone. "It's not nine thirty yet."

Dad opened the closet door, and I could hear the wooden hangers clattering together as he got out his jacket. "I have a busy day lined up, and I'm already getting a late start to drive you. Run next door and get Tyler. Let's go."

I took one last look at Tyler's porch, then hopped off the chair and joined my dad in the front hall, taking the jacket he handed me and putting it on. We went down the porch stairs toward the car, but I walked as slowly as I could to try to stretch out the minutes.

Dad stopped halfway to the driveway and looked over his shoulder at me. "Come on, Kat," he said impatiently, then frowned. "What about Tyler?"

My eyes darted toward his house again, hoping he would come out that second. Or the next . . . or maybe . . . Nope. He wasn't coming.

"Oh, uh . . . he's getting a ride there separately."

The lines in Dad's forehead got a little deeper, but he didn't say anything as he hit the button on his key chain to unlock the car. I walked around the other side and opened the door, pausing as I looked at Tyler's front door one last time.

Please come out now, I said in my head.

"Kat, let's go," Dad said, really impatient now, so I scrambled into the car and buckled up.

We were only a half a block into the drive when Dad turned off the radio. "Want to tell me what's going on?"

"What do you mean?" I asked, as if I had no idea what he was talking about.

"You and Tyler."

"Oh. Uh, no, I don't want to tell you about it."

Apparently, when he'd asked if I wanted to tell him about it, it wasn't actually a question, because he just kept going on. "Does it have something to do with you leaving the dance on your own Friday night and then walking home alone?"

"Maybe. But I don't want to talk about it."

Sometimes dads don't care what you don't want to talk about. Especially when they have you trapped in their car. "Did you get into a fight?"

He obviously wasn't going to let it go. I sighed.

"Okay, yes, we got into a fight. Well, actually, I did something stupid and now he hates my guts."

I could see out of the corner of my eye that Dad took his eyes off the road to look at me, but I kept my eyes trained out the front windshield.

"What did you do?" he asked.

"It's stupid. Can we not talk about it?"

"Kat," he said. "I know I'm old and your dad, but maybe I can help."

"I doubt it," I said.

He chuckled. "I may have been down this road once or twice. I've done some stupid things in relationships before and I—"

"We're *NOT* in a *relationship*!"

"Whoa," Dad said, holding up a palm. "Relax. Friendships count as relationships. What I meant was that I might be able to offer some insight."

I didn't say anything.

"Tell me what happened," he said softly.

I was super embarrassed, but maybe he *could* help. I mean, we were on the way to the shelter, and Tyler wasn't talking to me. What did I have to lose?

"Fine. Olivia liked him, but he wasn't into her because she likes boy bands and dancing and hair and stuff and he likes books and games and manga."

"Right, of course," Dad said.

I looked over, but he wasn't smirking, so I went on. "So she pretended she was into all the things he likes."

"Okaaaaaay," he said. "So how does this involve you?"

I was suddenly worried that admitting to tricking Tyler might get me into more trouble with my parents. My stomach rolled the toast around again, but I realized that if there were consequences, I probably deserved them. "Uh . . . I *may have* been secretly on the phone with her while she was talking to him and told her what to say."

"*May have . . .*"

"And I *may have* pretended to be her when we played Zombie Slashers remotely."

"Right. What else?"

"Uh, I *may have* tried to whisper lines to her at the dance from under the bleachers."

He smirked at that but quickly straightened out his

mouth just as I was going to tell him that none of this was funny. "Well, no one can say you're not resource-ful," he said when his face was serious again.

"Maybe. But *stupid*. He caught us." I began to chew on my thumbnail.

"And I'm guessing he wasn't flattered by all the effort you two put into this elaborate scheme?"

"Not exactly," I said. "Like I said: hates my guts."

"I doubt that," Dad said as he turned onto the free-way. "You two have been friends for a long time. I'm sure he's hurt that you were dishonest with him. But he'll come around."

I sighed and pulled my thumb away from my mouth; I'd already bitten the nail all the way down. Any more and I might be considered a cannibal. "I don't think so, Dad. He was pretty angry."

"You'll have to apologize, obviously."

"I tried. He won't answer my texts."

"Maybe corner him at the shelter? Lock him in a kennel and pour your heart out to him?"

I rolled my eyes. "Hilarious."

Dad smiled at me for a second and then looked

back at the road. "Listen, Kat. Here's a bit of tough love. Relationships—friendships, love relationships, whatever—they take work, and people make mistakes. It's easy to lose sight of the endgame sometimes, but it doesn't just happen; you have to work at it."

"What's the endgame?"

"That you want to have that person in your life. That you care about them, and sometimes that means putting them first, ahead of yourself or your own wants."

That made sense. Neither Olivia nor I had really thought about Tyler's feelings in all of this. I guess I'd thought he'd be happy to be with her in the end, but if I'd *really* thought about him and what he'd want, I would have known better.

But as I thought about what my dad was saying, I also thought about my family. All the nights we waited for *him* to come home, and then how when he *was* home, he was crabby and distracted or sleeping on the couch.

"Dad?" I said.

"Yeah?"

"Um . . ."

He looked over. "What is it?"

"What you said . . . that makes a lot of sense."

He smiled and turned into the shelter parking lot. "But . . . uh . . ."

We drove around back to the staff parking, and he took a spot near the back door. Once the car was stopped, he turned it off and looked at me. "What?"

I swallowed, nervous about what I was going to say. But I needed to say it. "That putting-other-people-first thing . . . I don't think you do that with Mom or Laura and me. You've been working so much lately, we hardly see you."

His face fell, and I suddenly felt like the worst person in the world (as if I didn't already) for making him upset. "Kat, you know this new practice—"

"I know, Dad. We understand. Sort of. But does it have to be so much? We miss you, and some days . . ." My throat got really tight choking out the words.

Dad took my hand in his big, warm one. "Kat? Some days what?"

"Some days Mom looks *really* sad."

He was quiet for so long that I had to look up at him.

His eyes looked sad now, and I had to glance away or I was going to start bawling. "I'm sorry," I whispered.

He squeezed my hand. "No, don't be sorry. You're one hundred percent right. I haven't been putting my family first. That stops today."

"Really?" I asked.

"Really," he said, tugging my hand. "Undo your seat belt so you can give me a hug."

I clicked the button and laughed when my dad pulled me into his arms. He squished me so tight I almost couldn't breathe.

"Let me go," I said.

"In a minute," he said, but then did let me go after a final squeeze. "I'm so sorry, Kat."

I shrugged. "We all make mistakes, right?"

"Where did you get all your smarts from?" he asked, smirking at me.

"Mom, obviously."

He rolled his eyes. "Come on, we'd better get inside. Let's see if we can fix this thing with Tyler, too."

Ugh. Something told me that was going to be a lot harder than giving my father a dose of tough love.

Chapter 21

AS WE GOT OUT OF THE CAR, I TRIED TO TAKE A deep breath to calm my nerves. I desperately wanted to see Tyler but was at the same time completely terrified to see him. I know that seems crazy, but my brain was all jumbled with stress over what had happened, and I was so worried he'd never forgive me. Dad seemed to think he would; I just hoped he was right.

He pulled the door open, letting out the sounds of dogs barking. We walked down the hallway until we got to a doorway marked AUTHORIZED PERSONNEL ONLY, and Dad stopped. "I'll be back in the clinic doing surgeries for most of the day, but come get me when you're done, all right?"

I nodded. "Okay."

He gave me a quick side hug. "It'll be fine."

"Thanks, Dad," I said, secretly thankful for the hug and the little pep talk. He left me there in the hall, so I took a deep breath and headed down to sign in and get my badge. I suddenly worried that Tyler hadn't come at all. Maybe he wanted to avoid me so badly that he'd bail on volunteering.

Yet with each step I realized more and more that he wouldn't do that. Tyler is the kind of person who doesn't bail on things, no matter how uncomfortable.

So when I got to the desk and signed in, I wasn't surprised to see his name on the line above where I put mine.

"Your friend beat you in this morning," Justine said as she walked up to the desk. "Sorry, but that means you're on kennel duty today."

I nodded, feeling like I deserved to clean up poop after what I'd done to Tyler. "He's already out walking?" I asked.

"Yep, got here early," she said. "He's a nice boy."

"He sure is," I agreed, putting down the pen and taking my badge from her hand.

"You know where everything is?" Justine asked.

I nodded and put on my badge.

"Don't forget the rubber boots," she said.

If I hadn't already been somewhat convinced that Tyler hated me, four hours later I *totally* was. He'd come and gone several times, taking dogs out for walks while I cleaned kennels, and not once had he even looked at me, let alone talked to me. I tried to catch his eye a couple of times, but it was obvious he was avoiding me, so I gave up, throwing myself into cleaning.

Tyler put away his last dog of the day as I was removing the rubber boots, goggles, and smock. I took my time, not wanting to run into him at the volunteer desk as we signed out and handed back our badges. By the time I went out there, he was gone, so I finished up and then went to find my dad. We left by the back door and drove around the building, where Tyler was standing at the bus stop.

"Isn't that Tyler?" Dad asked.

"Yes."

"It didn't go well, I presume."

"He hates my guts."

Without another word Dad pulled to the end of the lot—right at the street, so that Tyler was just a few feet from my side of the car—and pushed the button to make my window go down.

"What are you doing?" I sputtered at Dad, but he decided not to hear me.

He leaned toward me instead. "Tyler!" he yelled out the window. "Come on, get in."

Tyler shook his head. "It's okay. I'll take the bus."

"Aren't you going home?" Dad said.

"He said he was going to take the bus," I said quietly without moving my lips or taking my eyes off the windshield in front of me.

"Yeah. It's okay, though," Tyler said.

"Don't be silly," my father—the most infuriating man on the planet—said. "Get in. We don't bite."

I might bite you, I thought. But then, as I sat there holding my breath, I saw out of the corner of my eye when Tyler realized he was beat. He trudged toward the car and opened the door behind me.

"Thanks," Tyler said. Of course, his voice made it obvious that the last place in the world he wanted to be was in the car with me.

"How was your day today?" Dad asked. I was thankful that he was at least willing to make conversation with Tyler, since he had made this the most awkward drive ever.

"Pretty good. I walked a lot of dogs."

"Did you take Daisy out? The Jack Russell mix?"

"Yeah."

"How's that back leg?"

"She was limping a little, but it didn't seem to slow her down."

I sat there and listened to them talk about the different dogs, and then they switched to football for a while. I kept my mouth shut, because the more they talked, the less tense Tyler seemed to be. In fact, by the time we pulled into our driveway, he sounded almost normal. At least until we got out of the car.

Dad practically sprinted for the front door. I knew

he was leaving us alone so we could talk. Once he disappeared inside the house, I called out Tyler's name; but he was halfway to his own door.

He froze and then slowly turned back to face me. Okay, so his not completely ignoring me was a good sign. Score one for Kat.

"Can we talk about what happened?" I said, walking across the lawn toward him.

He pursed his lips.

"Please? I need to tell you—"

He held up his hand to stop me.

"No, Kat. I don't think so."

"But we're best friends," I said, my voice squeaky.

"Best friends don't trick each other. Best friends don't do what you did." He shook his head. "I can't talk to you. Not now, Kat."

As I stood there, he walked away from me. Again.

Chapter 22

ABOUT AN HOUR LATER I WAS SITTING AT THE desk in the kitchen, furiously working on *Hector: Ninja Cat* to try to get my mind off Tyler, when Dad came along and put his hand on my shoulder. "Your mom and I are going out to a movie. We'd invite you, but you're still grounded."

I wasn't in the mood to go to a movie anyway, but I was glad that Dad was spending the rest of the afternoon with Mom. "Okay. Have fun."

"Laura did laundry earlier, so you're on deck to do some raking this afternoon. Leaf bags are in the shed."

"Okay," I said.

"Sorry about Tyler," Dad said. "I tried. I hoped he'd come around."

I stared down at my artwork and shrugged, not sure what else to say.

"Keep at him. He just needs some time to start missing you, and then he'll let you explain you never meant to hurt him."

"I guess."

"You ready?" Mom asked as she came into the kitchen with her jacket on and her purse over her shoulder. She had a smile on her face, making me glad I'd worked up the courage to talk to Dad.

"Sure am," Dad said. "I was just letting Kat know about the leaves."

"Okay, let's go. We'll bring home dinner after," Mom said, looking at me. "How does Thai sound?"

"Great. Sweet soy noodles, please," I said, suddenly feeling a little better. I loved Thai food almost as much as I loved pizza.

Dad gave my shoulder one last squeeze. "See you later, Kat. By the way, your comic looks great. Just don't get caught up in it—those leaves won't rake themselves."

"Thanks," I said, flushing at his compliment, and pushed back from the desk as I heard them leave. He was right to worry that I might get caught up in working on my manga. Best to get my chore out of the way.

I grabbed a hoodie and put it on before I made my way out the back to the shed. I collected the rake and the big paper bags to stuff the leaves into and then slipped on a pair of gardening gloves as I surveyed the yard. Most of the leaves came from the big oak tree, the one between my house and Tyler's. I started on the far side of the backyard and made my way toward the tree, dragging the leaves over into a pile under the mostly empty branches.

I thought about my manga as I raked, working out the illustrations that would go along with the story, and was surprised when, a while later, I looked down at what was now a huge pile of leaves sitting under the tree. I had a sudden urge to text Tyler to come out so we could jump in the pile from our favorite low branch. Except that he wouldn't answer my text if I did.

I pulled my phone out of my jeans pocket just in case, but there was only one message from Olivia asking something about our homework. I messaged her and said I'd get back to her after I was done in the yard, then slipped the phone back in my pocket.

As I grabbed the handle of the rake again, I looked up and noticed Tyler's bedroom window was open a little. I thought about climbing the tree and yelling at him until he came to the window, but that didn't seem like a great idea. Still, I had to figure out a way to get him to listen to me and understand that I was sorry. Dad had said to give him time, but I didn't want to wait: What if he forgot about how we used to be best friends before I'd screwed everything up?

As I stared up, I suddenly had the best idea.

Chapter 23

IT HAD BEEN A WHILE SINCE I'D CLIMBED THE TREE, but my hands still seemed to remember where all the best branches were, and I was up to the big one near Tyler's window in no time. I secured myself, slid my backpack off my shoulders, and opened it to take out the envelope containing a page of *Hector: Ninja Cat*. It was my very best illustration, and a tiny part of me didn't want to give it up, but most of me was okay with it if it meant I would get my best friend back. When I'd taken the page out of my book, I'd planned to write my apology on the illustration, but thought better of it and instead wrote it on a big sticky note, then slid it all into one of Dad's big envelopes.

I hung the backpack on a smaller branch and shimmied over toward Tyler's window. I couldn't see him in the room, but his bed was against the outside wall, so he could have been sitting there and I wouldn't have known. I took a deep breath and leaned toward the window, as close as I safely could. Then I reached out and pushed the envelope through the opening. I waited for what felt like hours to see if Tyler would retrieve it, but I didn't hear a sound, so either he was still ignoring me or he wasn't in his room.

With a sigh I grabbed my backpack, put it over my shoulders, and started down the tree again. I stopped at the last big branch, took out my phone, and opened up a message to him.

Kat: *there's something in your room. Please look at it.*

Tyler: . . .

I sat there on the branch waiting for his message to finish until my butt got so sore that I couldn't stand it. Then I put the phone away and dropped into the big pile of leaves, trying not to scatter them too much, since I'd just have to rake them up again.

Jumping in leaves is no fun to do on your own.

I took off my backpack and put it just inside the back door so I could return to my raking.

"Kat?"

I whipped around to see Tyler standing there, his hands in his jeans pockets, a weird look on his face.

He didn't look mad, but he wasn't exactly smiling, either. I wasn't sure what to say, but his name slipped out of my mouth. "Ty . . ."

"I liked your drawing," he said. "It looks good. No, not just good—really *amazing*."

"Thanks," I said, loving that he thought so.

"Um . . ."

I just stared at him, holding my breath as I waited for him to say whatever was coming next.

"I . . . So I read your note."

"I really am sorry," I blurted out, because I couldn't wait one more second. "We . . . I . . . it was stupid what we did, and the last thing I meant to do was hurt you or make you mad at me."

He nodded. "I just don't understand why you

wanted me to be with her so bad that you would lie."

I shrugged, feeling my face getting really hot, but I simply couldn't tell him the truth. I would die before admitting that I'd thought getting them together would get rid of my crush on him, that we could go back to being just friends. Anyway, as I stood there, looking at the leaves under my shoes, I realized that getting him together with Olivia *never* would have made my crush go away—how stupid had I been to think for a second that it would have?

"I don't know," I said, kicking a few leaves toward the pile. "It made sense at the time. I thought you'd like her. She's the kind of girl all guys like."

He exhaled and looked away. "Don't you get it, Kat?"

"Don't I get what?"

He cleared his throat. And then he coughed and cleared his throat a second time. I was about to ask him if he needed a cough drop or something when he blurted out, "I like *you*."

I opened my mouth, but nothing came out as I stared at him, his words sinking in.

He still hadn't looked at me, but his eyes were now trained on the ground. His voice was quiet when he said, "Did you hear me?"

"I don't think so," I said. "You'd better say it again."

His face was really pink as he came toward me. "I can't believe you thought for a second that I'd pick her over you, and then you even tried to make her *into* you."

Was that what I'd done? "But she's so tall. And pretty. And bubbly."

"She's not you," he said. He was coming so close; if it had been anyone else, I would have stepped away. But it wasn't anyone else. It was him.

"She's graceful and doesn't have glasses or braces."

"She isn't you," he repeated, his eyes on mine.

"You like *me*?" I whispered.

He snorted. "How many times do I have to say it?"

"I don't know. Maybe once more."

He smiled, his eyes dropping away from mine. "Do *you* like *me*, Kat?"

My heart was racing in my chest, and it was hard to breathe, but the dread I'd felt when I'd thought he hated my guts was replaced with a jittery, giddy feeling—like the time my parents told us we were going to Disney World.

"Yes," I said. "I do like you."

"More than a friend?" he asked, eyes still facing the ground.

"I don't know," I said.

He looked up at me, and his face sort of fell. "What?"

"I don't know what that's supposed to feel like," I said, confused. "I mean, I want to be best friends again and play Zombie Slashers and talk manga and books with you, more than anything. But that's friends, isn't it?"

"*Best* friends," he said. "But . . . do you *like* me like me?"

"I think so," I said. "Maybe I don't know the difference."

He leaned forward and grabbed my hand. It was kind of like when we were dancing, but a million times better: He was holding my hand because he *wanted* to (plus, my mom wasn't watching). I noticed that his hand wasn't as sweaty this time. It felt nice. Weird and a bit scary, but mostly really nice. I thought about Olivia, and how holding her hand would never, *ever* feel like this.

I was suddenly very, very sure. "Okay, I think I understand now. And yes, I *like* you like you."

"Good," Tyler said, grinning as he squeezed my hand and pulled me closer. "I can't wait to beat my *girlfriend* at Zombie Slashers."

I laughed. "You can *try* to beat your girlfriend at Zombie Slashers."

"Looking forward to it," he said right before he leaned forward and gave me a kiss on my cheek. It was actually almost my ear, so I heard it more than felt it, but I hadn't expected it and leaned back away from him.

"Sorry," he said, suddenly looking panicked.

"It's okay," I said, my face heating up because it was very okay that he'd kissed me, but it was still a little embarrassing. "I was just surprised, and it was kind of loud, that's all."

"Right," he said, that piece of hair falling over his

forehead distractingly. "Maybe I should try it again?"

I nodded. "You should definitely try it again," I said. "But first I need to finish these leaves or I'm going to be in big trouble. I'm already grounded."

Tyler let go of my one hand and took the rake from the other as he grinned at me. "We'd better get started, then, Kat," he said as he started raking.

"I like the way you think, Ty," I said, grabbing a leaf bag to hold open for my best friend—er . . . *boy*friend.

Acknowledgments

SOME PEOPLE SAY THAT WRITING ACKNOWLEDG-ments for a book is harder than writing the actual book. Those some people are right. I have so many people to thank for everything that has led to you holding this book in your hands and I have done a lot of worrying to make sure I haven't missed anyone, so hopefully I haven't.

Starting with the people who very directly made this book happen, beginning with Caryn Wiseman, who is truly a hardworking and clever agent—thank you for your faith in me and your tireless efforts.

To Amy Cloud, who took a chance on me and has been an amazing editor from day one (and who totally gets me, even at my dorkiest), my most heartfelt thanks. Another thank-you to the other fine folks at Simon & Schuster (NY): Mandy Veloso, Sarah Kwak,

Laura Lyn DiSiena, Karen Sherman, and artist Angela Li, who illustrated the cutest cover ever, right down to Ty's mysterious hair! Another shout-out to the folks at Simon & Schuster Canada, who love their local authors (and it shows!).

This book is dedicated to my parents and for good reason: I can't imagine having two more supportive and loving parents had I handpicked them. They always told me that I could be whatever I wanted to be, and it seems they were right. Except for that time I told them what I wanted was to be a pony owner. Still, they were both integral in giving me the tools to work hard, be persistent, and reach for the stars. Though my mom isn't here anymore, I know she's out there somewhere, talking to anyone who will listen about her daughter, the published author.

A huge thank-you to my constant support and biggest cheerleader, my husband, Deke. Thank you for the plot assistance, encouragement, and never-ending belief in me. You are an amazing partner and I am so honored to be your Team Snow cocaptain.

For my early readers of this book: Joyce Grant,